T.S. DUNNE

Silver Siren

Secrets Investigation

First edition

This book was professionally typeset on Reedsy.
Find out more at reedsy.com

Contents

1

Vanishing Shadows: Shannon's Curiosity Ignites

Shannon stood in front of the camera, her heart pounding with a mix of excitement and determination. The breaking news report she was about to deliver would capture the attention of viewers across Malibu, and she knew that this was her chance to dive deep into the mysterious disappearance of her former high school classmate, Raymond Fitzgerald.

Her voice filled the airwaves as she began, her words precise and measured. "Good evening, Malibu. I'm Shannon Saunders, and tonight we bring you a developing story that has left our community on edge. Raymond Fitzgerald, a beloved member of our tight-knit community, has vanished without a trace."

As Shannon spoke, the camera panned over the newsroom behind her, a whirlwind of activity. Reporters huddled together, frantically typing on their keyboards, while producers barked out orders and directed the flow of information. The urgency in their movements mirrored Shannon's own determination to uncover the truth.

Raymond's disappearance hit close to home for Shannon. She had known him since their high school days, and even though they had taken different paths after graduation, his absence haunted her. The memories of their shared laughter and inside jokes flooded her mind as she spoke into the camera.

"Raymond and I were classmates at Malibu High School," she continued, her voice tinged with emotion. "We laughed together, cried together, and dreamed of our futures side by side. But now, he has vanished into thin air, leaving behind a void in our lives."

The fiery red waves of Shannon's hair floored viewers as they stared at their screens. Her piercing blue eyes held a fierce determination that captivated audiences, drawing them deeper into the story. Her commitment to her role as an investigative reporter shone through every word she uttered.

As Shannon's voiceover narrated the details of Raymond's disappearance, images flashed across the screen—photographs of Raymond as a carefree teenager, his infectious smile lighting up the frame. The juxtaposition of those memories with the stark reality of his disappearance struck a chord in the hearts of viewers.

In her newsroom, Shannon's colleagues paused for a moment, their eyes glued to the monitors displaying her report. They knew that she had a knack for unraveling the truth, for peeling back the layers until she uncovered the core of a story. And this time, Raymond's story was hers to tell.

The scene ended, and as the camera turned off, Shannon took a deep breath. She could feel the weight of responsibility on her shoulders, but it only fueled her determination to find answers. Raymond's disappearance was no longer just a news story—it had become a personal mission, a quest to uncover the truth behind his vanishing act.

Little did Shannon know that by delving into Raymond's case, she would open doors to a world she never imagined—one steeped in mystery, therapy, and hallucinations. As she stepped away from the camera, ready to embark on her investigation, she couldn't help but wonder where this journey would lead her—and what secrets it would ultimately unveil.

Shannon couldn't help but feel a nostalgic pang in her chest as she walked through the hallways of her old high school. The sound of lockers slamming and laughter echoing down the corridor brought back a flood of memories from her teenage years. She had spent countless hours here, navigating the complexities of friendship, young love, and the insecurities that came with growing up.

Her purpose for returning to Malibu High School wasn't purely sentimental though. Shannon had a mission - to gather any information she could about Raymond Fitzgerald's mysterious disappearance. As she made her way towards the main courtyard, she felt a mix of anticipation and unease. She knew that revisiting these memories might unearth painful truths, but she was willing to face them for the sake of solving Raymond's case.

The courtyard was filled with students enjoying their lunch break, their voices blending together in a cacophony of chatter. Shannon spotted Blaise, her former boyfriend and friend of Raymond, surrounded by a group of fellow classmates. His vibrant personality drew people towards him like a magnet.

With determination written across her face, Shannon approached the group. "Blaise! It's been ages since we last saw each other," she exclaimed, a touch of warmth in her voice.

Blaise turned around, a smile lighting up his face as recognition dawned upon him. "Shannon! I can't believe it's you." He reached out for a quick embrace before gesturing to his friends. "These are my buddies. Remember Doug and Emily?"

Shannon nodded, greeting them with a polite smile. Memories of shared adventures flooded back as they exchanged light-hearted banter. They reminisced about high school pranks, outrageous parties, and the trouble they used to get into.

All the while, Shannon subtly probed for any information related to Raymond's disappearance without raising suspicion. She asked questions about their last interactions with him, his state of mind, and any unusual behavior they might have noticed.

As the conversation continued, Shannon's keen observation skills picked up on subtle hints of tension between Blaise and his friends. At times, their voices would lower to whispers before quickly shifting back to cheerful banter. It was as if they were guarding a secret, something they weren't ready to reveal just yet.

Shannon's heart pounded in her chest as she sensed a breakthrough. She couldn't shake the feeling that Blaise held a crucial piece of information about Raymond's disappearance. She recalled the last time she had seen them together, sharing laughs and dreams for the future. But now, that future seemed uncertain, clouded by unanswered questions.

With each passing minute, Shannon's determination grew stronger. She knew she had stumbled upon a thread that could lead her closer to unraveling the truth. As the lunch bell rang, signaling the end of the break, Shannon exchanged contact information with Blaise and his friends, promising to meet again soon.

Walking away from Malibu High School, Shannon's mind raced with possibilities. She knew that revisiting her high school memories had unearthed something important - a potential lead in Raymond's disappearance. It was a small victory, but one that filled her with renewed hope.

As she got into her car and drove away, Shannon couldn't help but wonder what other secrets lay hidden beneath the surface of their seemingly idyllic coastal town. Raymond's disappearance was just the beginning of a puzzle waiting to be solved. And with every step she took closer to finding the truth, Shannon became acutely aware that there was much more at stake than she had initially realized.

2

Unraveling Shadows

Shannon stood outside Raymond's childhood home, her hand poised to ring the doorbell. The memories of their shared laughter and adventures came flooding back, intertwining with the anticipation that hung heavy in the air. The plain exterior of the house seemed weathered by time, a silent witness to Raymond's past.

Taking a deep breath, Shannon rang the doorbell. Moments later, the door creaked open, revealing Mr. and Mrs. Fitzgerald, Raymond's parents. Their faces were etched with a mixture of gratitude and desperation as they welcomed Shannon inside. The musty scent of old memories filled the air, mingling with unspoken grief.

In the living room, family photographs adorned the walls, capturing moments frozen in time. Shannon's eyes scanned the room, searching for any detail that might offer insight into Raymond's disappearance. Each photograph told a story of joy and togetherness, casting an air of warmth and nostalgia over the room.

As they settled into conversation, Shannon listened intently as Mr. and Mrs. Fitzgerald recounted fond memories of their son. They described his infectious laughter, his love for adventure, and his unwavering loyalty to those he cared about. Shannon's sharp observation skills analyzed their words, searching for hidden emotions beneath their somber tone.

With gentle persistence, Shannon asked about Raymond's state of mind before his disappearance. Mrs. Fitzgerald glanced at her husband, her eyes welling with tears. "Raymond seemed troubled," she confessed. "He withdrew from his friends and family in the weeks leading up to his disappearance. We tried to reach out to him, but he always insisted he was fine."

Mr. Fitzgerald joined in, his voice filled with anguish. "We thought it was just teenage angst, you know? But now... now we fear there was something more going on. Something we couldn't see."

Shannon leaned forward, her eyes locked onto theirs. "Is there anything else you can tell me? Anything that might provide a clue as to where Raymond might have gone?"

A heavy silence settled over the room, pregnant with unspoken secrets. Mrs. Fitzgerald sighed, her eyes filled with a mixture of pain and hope. "There was something... peculiar," she admitted hesitantly. "Raymond recently became involved in a therapy group that used a unique approach involving psilocybin."

Psilocybin therapy. The words hung in the air, igniting a spark of intrigue within Shannon. She had come across mentions of it in her research, but the connection to Raymond's disappearance sent a jolt of excitement through her. It was controversial, yet believed by some to hold the key to unlocking buried memories and healing emotional trauma.

"What do you know about this therapy?" Shannon asked, her voice steady despite her racing thoughts.

Mr. Fitzgerald shook his head, regret etched on his face. "We didn't know much at first. It was just another desperate attempt to help Raymond deal with his struggles. But now... now we fear it may have led him down a dangerous path."

Shannon's mind raced with possibilities, connecting the dots between psilocybin therapy and Raymond's sudden disappearance. Had he unlocked something during those sessions that put him in harm's way? The thought churned in her mind, fueling her determination to uncover the truth.

With resolve burning in her eyes, Shannon turned back to Raymond's parents. "I promise you, Mr. and Mrs. Fitzgerald, I will do everything in my power to find your son and bring him home. No stone will be left unturned."

Their gratitude was palpable, their faith in Shannon unwavering. As she left Raymond's childhood home, her mind buzzed with new leads and unanswered questions. Psilocybin therapy had become a pivotal point of her investigation, and she knew that delving deeper into this world would unveil secrets that had remained hidden for far too long.

The journey ahead was perilous, but Shannon embraced it with unwavering resolve. She would follow the path of psilocybin therapy, hoping it would lead her to Raymond and uncover the truth behind his disappearance. Little did she know the dangers that lay ahead, for unraveling the silver siren's secrets would test not only her investigative skills but also her own strength and resilience.

3

Unveiling the Enigmatic Therapy

Shannon sat in her dimly lit office, surrounded by stacks of scientific articles and academic journals. The room had become her sanctuary, a haven where she could unravel the mysteries surrounding psilocybin therapy. Her desk was cluttered with stacks of research, each one holding the potential to reveal a crucial piece of the puzzle.

The sound of flipping pages filled the air as Shannon's piercing blue eyes scanned the words before her. She absorbed every detail with unwavering focus, her mind absorbing knowledge like a sponge. The realm of psilocybin therapy unfolded before her, its intricacies and possibilities weaving together in her mind.

As Shannon read through study after study, a tapestry of understanding began to take shape. Psilocybin, a naturally occurring hallucinogenic compound found in certain mushrooms, held the potential for profound healing and self-discovery. It was believed to unlock hidden memories and facilitate therapeutic breakthroughs, but it also carried risks that needed to be carefully considered.

The voices of experts echoed in Shannon's mind, their wisdom leading her down a path of discovery. They spoke of altered states of consciousness, guiding patients through their deepest fears and traumas, and the delicate balance between healing and potential risks. Each word resonated within her, fueling her determination to uncover the truth behind Raymond's disappearance.

Hours turned into days as Shannon dove deeper into the labyrinthine world of psilocybin therapy. But just when she felt she couldn't absorb any more information, fate intervened. In the midst of her research, she stumbled upon a hidden journal tucked away among Raymond's personal belongings.

Curiosity danced in Shannon's eyes as she delicately turned the yellowed pages. The faded ink revealed cryptic entries, each one a glimpse into Raymond's involvement in an underground therapeutic community centered around psilocybin. Her heart quickened with excitement. Could this journal hold the missing pieces of the puzzle? Would it unveil Raymond's whereabouts and the truth of his connection to psilocybin therapy?

Time seemed to stand still as Shannon immersed herself in Raymond's words. He spoke of profound experiences, of visions that felt more real than reality itself, and of a journey that had stirred something deep within him. These revelations ignited Shannon's determination, propelling her forward on her quest for answers.

In the dimly lit room, Shannon lost herself in the pages of the journal, her mind whirling with possibilities. She knew that these discoveries would take her down a dangerous path, testing not only her investigative skills but also her own sanity. Yet, she couldn't ignore the burning desire within her to unravel the secrets of the silver siren.

As she read on, Shannon could sense the weight of responsibility settling upon her shoulders. The lives of those seeking healing through psilocybin therapy, as well as the truth behind Raymond's disappearance, rested in her hands. With each word she absorbed, she grew closer to understanding the power of this unique therapy and its potential dangers.

The clock on Shannon's desk ticked relentlessly, reminding her that time was slipping away. But in that moment, all that mattered was the world contained within the journal and the whispers of truth waiting to be unveiled. With renewed vigor, she delved deeper into its faded pages, determined to bring Raymond back home and shed light on the enigmatic world of psilocybin therapy.

As Shannon emerged from her office, an aura of determination surrounded her like a protective shield. She would follow the path forged by Raymond, unraveling the silver siren's secrets one page at a time. The journey ahead was treacherous and uncertain, but Shannon was ready to face whatever challenges awaited her.

With every step she took, Shannon could feel the weight of responsibility deepening. The lives of those who sought solace in psilocybin therapy depended on her ability to uncover the truth. And as she ventured further into the unknown, she knew that the secrets she would uncover had the power to change lives.

The world of psilocybin therapy awaited Shannon, beckoning her with its promises of healing and enlightenment. But beneath the surface, danger lurked, ready to ensnare those who ventured too far. Yet, Shannon's resolve remained unshakable. She would forge ahead, guided by curiosity and fueled by a burning desire for justice.

As she stepped into the unknown, Shannon's fiery red hair seemed to shimmer with determination. She was ready to face the challenges that lay ahead, armed with knowledge and emboldened by the truth she sought. The journey would be arduous, but Shannon was no longer alone. Raymond's journal held the key to understanding his disappearance, and together they would unveil the silver siren's secrets.

And so, Shannon embarked on her mission, weaving through a tangle of deception and perilous paths. Each step brought her closer to the answers she sought, but also deeper into a world fraught with danger. Nothing could deter her from bringing Raymond home and shedding light on the enigmatic realm of psilocybin therapy.

The journey that lay ahead would test Shannon's investigative skills and challenge her own resilience. But in the face of uncertainty, she remained steadfast, her determination unwavering. With each turn of the page and every revelation uncovered,

Shannon drew closer to unraveling the silver siren's secrets and discovering the truth that had eluded her for so long.

4

Rekindling Flames

A Chance Encounter

Shannon entered the bustling coffee shop in downtown Malibu, the rich aroma of freshly brewed coffee enveloping her senses. The air hummed with the sound of animated conversations and the clinking of coffee cups against saucers. Baristas hustled behind the counter, expertly crafting each order with a practiced precision. It was the kind of place where people gathered to fuel their caffeine cravings and seek respite from the outside world.

As Shannon stood in line, waiting patiently for her turn to order, she absentmindedly perused the menu on the wall. Her finger traced the list of options, her mind wandering as she contemplated her choices. Lost in her thoughts, she didn't notice someone approaching from behind until she accidentally bumped into them.

Startled, Shannon turned around to apologize, ready to express her regret for the unintended collision. But as her gaze met the familiar face before her, her words caught in her throat. It was Blaise, her former high school boyfriend, his eyes widening in surprise mirroring Shannon's own astonishment.

"Shannon? Is that really you?" Blaise asked, his voice laced with disbelief.

A smile tugged at the corners of Shannon's lips as a wave of nostalgia washed over her. "Blaise," she replied, her voice tinged with a mixture of surprise and delight. "It's been... so long."

Blaise's face softened with a fondness that hadn't diminished over time. He reached out to pull Shannon into an embrace, and she willingly reciprocated, feeling a flood of memories resurface in that simple act. It was as if they had been transported back to their carefree days in high school, when life was filled with endless possibilities and dreams seemed within reach.

As they released each other from their embrace, they couldn't help but stare at one another, taking in the changes that time had wrought. Shannon's fiery red hair cascaded in loose waves around her face, matching the sparks of determination in her piercing blue eyes. Blaise, on the other hand, exuded a relaxed confidence, his carefree demeanor belying the wisdom that came with age.

They exchanged pleasantries, catching up on the major events that had transpired in their lives since they last saw each other. Careers had been pursued, relationships had bloomed and faded away, and life had taken its twists and turns. Yet, despite the passing years, there was an undeniable connection between them that lingered in the air, a thread that tied their hearts together despite the distance that had separated them.

As they continued to engage in small talk, Shannon couldn't help but feel a sense of serendipity in their chance encounter. It was almost as if the universe had conspired to bring them together at this precise moment in time. And though Shannon had initially entered the coffee shop seeking answers to Raymond's disappearance, she couldn't ignore the possibility that Blaise held valuable insights into their former classmate's whereabouts.

A mixture of hope and apprehension filled the air as Shannon contemplated how to broach the subject. She knew that she needed to tread carefully, respecting Blaise's boundaries while still conveying her desire for answers. But deep down, she couldn't shake off the nagging feeling that Blaise might hold a piece of the puzzle that would help unravel the mystery surrounding Raymond's sudden vanishing act.

As Shannon sipped her coffee and engaged in lighthearted banter with Blaise, her mind buzzed with questions. How well did Blaise know Raymond? Had they remained in contact after high school? And most importantly, what insights could he provide into Raymond's last known whereabouts?

The bustling coffee shop faded into the background as Shannon delved into her memories of Blaise and Raymond during their high school years. She couldn't shake off the feeling that reconnecting with Blaise might hold the key to unlocking the mysteries she sought.

Little did Shannon know, this chance encounter would set in motion a series of events that would lead her deeper into the shadows of Malibu, testing not only her investigative skills but also the bonds she had formed with those closest to her. With every word exchanged and every glance shared, Shannon's determination grew stronger. She was ready to uncover the truth behind Raymond's disappearance, no matter where it might lead.

Shannon suggested finding a quieter spot to continue their conversation, away from the hustle and bustle of the coffee shop. Blaise agreed, and together they made their way to a nearby park that overlooked the vast expanse of the ocean. The sound of crashing waves filled the air, creating a soothing backdrop for their discussion.

As they settled on a bench, Shannon allowed herself to take in the beauty of their surroundings. The sun cast a golden glow over the water, its rays reflecting off the crests of the waves. Seagulls swooped above, their cries mingling with the distant laughter of children playing on the beach.

With a nostalgic smile, Shannon began reminiscing about their shared memories from high school. She recounted their adventures and misadventures, reliving the moments that had shaped their teenage years. Blaise listened attentively, his eyes sparkling with recognition as he recalled their escapades.

"Do you remember that time we snuck out of school and went hiking up in the mountains?" Shannon asked with a chuckle. "We got completely lost and ended up having to rely on our wits to find our way back."

Blaise laughed, the sound rich and warm. "How could I forget? We thought we were invincible, exploring untouched trails and discovering hidden gems in nature. Those were some of the best times of my life."

Their conversation flowed effortlessly as they delved into more memories, each anecdote fueling their connection. They spoke of football games under Friday night lights, late-night bonfires on the beach, and stolen kisses in secluded corners of the school campus. It was a trip down memory lane that filled them both with nostalgia and a profound sense of gratitude for those fleeting moments of youth.

But amidst their laughter and fond recollections, there was an underlying current of seriousness. Blaise knew that Shannon had sought him out not just for a trip down memory lane but also to uncover the truth about Raymond's disappearance. And as their conversation ebbed and flowed, he sensed her unspoken questions hanging in the air.

Blaise paused for a moment, his face taking on a more pensive expression. "Shannon," he began, his voice laced with concern, "I heard about Raymond's disappearance. I wish I could say I knew something that could help, but all I have are fragments of memories and unanswered questions."

Shannon nodded, understanding the limitations of their shared history. "I figured as much," she replied softly. "But any insight you can provide, no matter how small, might be valuable in piecing together the puzzle. Did Raymond ever mention anything to you before he vanished? Anything that seemed out of the ordinary?"

Blaise sighed and ran a hand through his hair, his eyes fixed on the shimmering waters below. "He did," he admitted reluctantly. "Raymond confided in me about his struggles with anxiety and depression. It wasn't something he openly talked about with others, but he trusted me enough to share his innermost thoughts."

Shannon's heart sank at the revelation. She had suspected that Raymond's mental health might play a role in his disappearance, but hearing it confirmed stung nonetheless. She wondered what had pushed him to the brink, what events had unfolded in the shadows of his life that ultimately led him to vanish without a trace.

Their conversation took on a more serious tone as they explored the possible connections between Raymond's mental state and his fascination with psilocybin therapy. Blaise confessed that Raymond had grown increasingly withdrawn in the weeks leading up to his disappearance, seeking solace in solitary walks along the beach and long hours spent contemplating life's mysteries.

"It was like he was searching for something," Blaise mused. "Something just out of reach that he hoped would bring him peace."

Shannon listened intently, her mind buzzing with possibilities. She knew that Raymond's connection to psilocybin therapy ran deep, but she still had many unanswered questions. Did he participate in these therapies? And if so, how did they impact his mental state and ultimately his disappearance?

As the sun began its descent towards the horizon, casting a warm glow over their surroundings, Shannon and Blaise sat in companionable silence. It was as if the weight of their shared memories, their unspoken thoughts, and their hopes for the future hung in the air between them.

In that moment, Shannon realized that reconnecting with Blaise had served a purpose beyond simply catching up. He held valuable insights into Raymond's last known whereabouts and state of mind. And as they sat there, bathed in the golden light of the setting sun, Shannon couldn't help but feel a renewed sense of determination. She was closer than ever to unraveling the silver siren's secrets and uncovering the truth about Raymond's disappearance.

With a glimmer of hope igniting within her, Shannon knew that their journey had only just begun. The path ahead would be treacherous and uncertain, but together with Blaise by her side, they were ready to face whatever challenges awaited them.

5

The Enigmatic Mirage: Shannon dives into the depths of Raymond's hallucinations, pursuing the truth behind the elusive "Silver Siren".

A Haunting Melody

The room was shrouded in darkness, with the late afternoon sunlight struggling to penetrate through dusty windows. Shannon stood in the center, surrounded by shelves lined with forgotten knick-knacks and old furniture draped in white sheets. A sense of mystery and intrigue hung in the air as she gingerly picked up a box tucked away in the corner.

Curiosity got the better of her, and she lifted the lid, revealing an assortment of items – faded photographs, handwritten letters, and a weathered cassette tape. Her eyes were drawn to the tape, its label barely legible but still hinting at its mysterious contents.

With trembling hands, Shannon inserted the tape into an old

player collecting dust on a nearby shelf. As soon as the haunting melody started to play, she found herself transported to another realm. The ethereal music swirled around her, filling the room with its melancholic beauty.

In that moment, memories flooded back to Shannon's mind – memories of Raymond, their conversations, and his fascination with a figure he called the silver siren. She recalled vividly how he had described encountering her during his therapy sessions, how her voice whispered secrets only he could hear. The silver siren seemed to represent a manifestation of his deepest desires and fears.

As the music continued to weave its spell, Shannon's determination grew. She needed to find out if the silver siren was real or merely a figment of Raymond's troubled mind. The melody seemed to hold the answer – a key that could unlock the mysteries surrounding his disappearance.

The room faded into the background as Shannon closed her eyes, allowing the music to envelop her senses. Its ethereal quality sent shivers down her spine, evoking an undeniable sense of unease. But beneath that unease lay a nagging curiosity, pulling her deeper into the web of secrets that surrounded Raymond's vanishing act.

Lost in the haunting melody, Shannon's mind drifted back to a particular conversation she had with Raymond. He had spoken of the silver siren with an intensity that bordered on obsession. He would describe her flowing silver hair, her luminous eyes, and the allure of her voice that held him captive during his therapy sessions.

Raymond believed that encountering the silver siren opened a doorway to his subconscious, allowing him to confront hidden traumas and unravel the complexities of his troubled mind. But Shannon couldn't shake off the feeling that there was more to this story, something darker lurking beneath the surface.

As the last notes of the melody faded away, Shannon's eyes fluttered open. The room was once again bathed in dim light, and reality crashed back down upon her. She knew that she had to explore further, to delve into the twisted labyrinth of Raymond's psyche and uncover the truth behind his obsession with the silver siren.

A resolve burned within Shannon as she gently removed the tape from the player, carefully placing it back in its box. She clutched it tightly, knowing that it held a piece of the puzzle she desperately sought to solve.

With determined steps, Shannon left the dusty room behind, venturing out into a world of uncertainty and hidden secrets. The silver siren had captured Raymond's imagination, leading him down a path from which he never returned. Now it was up to Shannon to follow that path, to unravel the enigma of the silver siren and discover if she was merely a product of Raymond's imagination or a tangible force lurking in the shadows.

Shannon sat across from the renowned psychology professor in his cluttered office, surrounded by towering stacks of books and walls covered in research papers. The room exuded an atmosphere of intellectual curiosity, a space dedicated to deep contemplation and the unraveling of the human mind.

As they began their conversation, Shannon's eyes were drawn to the professor's animated gestures and attentive demeanor. His deep understanding of dreams and the subconscious mind was evident in his every word, weaving a captivating tapestry of knowledge.

"Archetypes," the professor explained, leaning forward slightly, "are deeply ingrained patterns that reside in the collective unconscious. They serve as symbols and representations of universal human experiences."

Shannon listened intently, her mind racing with questions about the silver siren and Raymond's connection to her. She marveled at the professor's ability to shed light on the complexities of the human psyche, offering insights into the hidden realms of the mind.

"What does the silver siren represent?" she finally asked, her voice filled with anticipation.

The professor leaned back in his chair, contemplating her question for a moment. "The silver siren," he began after a pause, "could be seen as an embodiment of unexplored aspects of our own psyches. She represents a longing for transformation, a yearning for self-discovery."

Shannon's heart skipped a beat as she digested his words. The silver siren had haunted Raymond's thoughts, guiding him through the labyrinth of his troubled mind. Now, it seemed that this ethereal figure held greater significance – she symbolized the uncharted territories within each individual seeking healing and wholeness.

"But," Shannon interjected, her voice tinged with uncertainty, "does she exist beyond the realm of imagination? Could she be real?"

The professor's gaze turned introspective as he considered Shannon's question. "Reality," he said softly, "is subjective. Each individual experiences their own version of reality, shaped by their beliefs and perceptions. If the silver siren holds a profound meaning for Raymond, then her existence within his reality is undeniably real."

Shannon nodded, absorbing his words. The line between imagination and reality had become blurred, and she couldn't help but wonder if there was more to the silver siren than met the eye. Her quest to uncover the truth about Raymond's disappearance had taken on a new dimension – one filled with symbolism and the uncharted depths of human consciousness.

As she left the professor's office, Shannon's thoughts whirled with newfound understanding. The silver siren was both a product of Raymond's troubled mind and a force that held the potential for healing and self-discovery. The journey ahead seemed even more daunting, yet she felt a renewed sense of purpose and determination.

She stepped out into the world, her footsteps echoing with a newfound conviction. The enigma of the silver siren beckoned her forward, its mysteries intertwining with her own search for truth. In this intricate dance between reality and imagination, Shannon knew that she had embarked on a path that would test her resolve and push her limits.

With every step forward, Shannon delved deeper into the enigmatic realm of the silver siren. She would navigate the treacherous waters of uncertainty, armed with knowledge and driven by an insatiable desire to unravel the secrets that tied Raymond to this elusive figure.

The professor's words lingered in her mind, fueling her determination. The silver siren may exist beyond the boundaries of conventional understanding, but Shannon was ready to confront her head-on. She would follow every lead, pursue every clue until she uncovered the truth behind Raymond's disappearance and the enigma of the silver siren.

Her journey had only just begun, and there were still many challenges to face. But with each new revelation, Shannon grew stronger, her resolve unwavering. The path ahead may be treacherous, but armed with knowledge and driven by a burning curiosity, she was ready to take on whatever awaited her.

As she walked into the fading daylight, Shannon felt a sense of purpose wash over her. The silver siren's secrets were within reach, and she would not rest until she unraveled them all. The journey into the depths of the human mind had just begun, and Shannon was prepared to face whatever lay ahead with unwavering resolve and insatiable curiosity.

Shannon found herself standing in the dimly lit room, surrounded by dusty shelves and old furniture. The air felt heavy with a sense of mystery and intrigue as she approached a small box tucked away in the corner. Curiosity danced in her eyes as she carefully lifted the lid, revealing a collection of forgotten items.

Among faded photographs and handwritten letters, Shannon's attention was drawn to a weathered cassette tape. Its label had become worn with time, but the words "The Silver Siren's Song" were still faintly visible. A shiver ran down her spine as she realized the significance of this discovery – it was a key that could unlock the secrets surrounding Raymond's disappearance.

With trembling hands, Shannon inserted the tape into an old player and pressed play. The haunting melody that filled the room sent chills down her spine, its ethereal quality evoking a mixture of unease and fascination. It was as if the music transported her to another realm, a world where reality and imagination intertwined.

As she closed her eyes and allowed the music to envelop her senses, memories flooded back to Shannon's mind. She recalled vivid conversations with Raymond, his voice filled with both awe and trepidation as he described encountering the silver siren during his therapy sessions. It was a figure that seemed to represent his deepest desires and fears, a manifestation of his troubled mind.

As the last notes of the melody faded away, Shannon opened her eyes and was brought back to the present. The room returned to its dimly lit state, and she clutched the tape tightly in her hand. Determination burned within her as she realized that she needed to explore further, to unravel the enigma of the silver siren and discover if she was merely a creation of Raymond's imagination or something more.

Leaving the room behind, Shannon stepped out into a world brimming with surrealistic masterpieces. The art gallery buzzed with anticipation as patrons admired paintings that blurred the line between reality and fantasy. Shannon found herself drawn to a section featuring large-scale artworks depicting ethereal women, their features melting into one another.

Lost in the vibrant colors and intricate details, Shannon's attention was caught by an enigmatic artist who stood beside her. There was something mysterious about him, as if he held secrets within his soul. Their conversation soon turned to the silver siren, and the artist spoke of the mysteries of the subconscious mind and the symbolism within his work.

Intrigued by the parallels between his paintings and Raymond's hallucinations, Shannon felt a deeper connection forming. The artist hinted at an unseen connection, a shared understanding of the silver siren's allure and its significance in unlocking hidden truths. With each word exchanged, Shannon's determination grew stronger – she knew she had to delve further into the symbolism and meaning behind the silver siren.

As Shannon left the art gallery, her mind buzzed with new-found understanding. The silver siren seemed to transcend the boundaries of human imagination, holding a deeper meaning for those who encountered her. The journey ahead appeared more daunting than ever, but Shannon was filled with a fiery resolve to uncover the truth that lay hidden within the enigmatic figure.

Days turned into nights as Shannon sought answers from experts in psychology. She arranged a meeting with a renowned professor specializing in dreams and the subconscious mind. In his cluttered office, surrounded by towering stacks of books, they delved into discussions about archetypes and the power of the human mind.

The professor's insights shed light on the significance of recurring symbols in dreams and hallucinations. He spoke of the silver siren as an embodiment of unexplored aspects of Raymond's psyche – a representation of his longing for transformation and self-discovery. Shannon absorbed his words like a sponge, her understanding deepening with every passing moment.

Armed with knowledge and driven by an insatiable curiosity, Shannon ventured further into the hidden online realms dedicated to the silver siren. She sifted through conversations and shared experiences, piecing together fragments of insights from those who claimed to have encountered her.

As she read each account, Shannon felt herself becoming entangled in the stories – tales of allure, darkness, and the price paid for falling under the silver siren's spell. The web of intrigue tightened around her, but she refused to be consumed.

The final piece of the scene fell into place as Shannon stumbled upon an interview featuring a reclusive artist who had experienced visions of the silver siren. Intrigued, she reached out to him for an interview, hoping to uncover more about their shared encounters.

In his secluded art studio, the artist revealed that the silver siren transcended the boundaries of imagination and represented a collective unconsciousness. She was more than a mere hallucination; she held profound meaning and potential dangers. With every revelation, Shannon's fascination and apprehension grew.

As she left the artist's studio, Shannon felt a renewed sense of purpose. The enigma surrounding Raymond's disappearance and the silver siren beckoned her forward. With each step, her determination burned brighter, her resolve unwavering.

The journey ahead would be treacherous and filled with unknown dangers, but Shannon was prepared to face whatever awaited her. The silver siren's allure had captivated many before her, but Shannon was armed with knowledge and driven by an unyielding curiosity. She would navigate the twisted web of mystery and danger until she unraveled the secrets that tied Raymond to this elusive figure.

With each breath, Shannon delved deeper into the mysteries surrounding Raymond's disappearance and his connection to the silver siren. The path before her was hidden in shadows, but fueled by determination and insatiable curiosity, she pressed forward.

The silver siren's secrets were within reach, and Shannon would not rest until she unraveled them all. The journey had only just begun, and she was prepared to face whatever challenges lay ahead. With every step she took, the silver siren's allure grew stronger, guiding her towards the truth that awaited her in the depths of the enigmatic world they shared.

6

Under the Moon's Glow

The darkness of the night embraced Shannon as she ventured further onto the Malibu Beach Pier, her steps cautious yet determined. With each step, the wooden planks beneath her feet creaked, harmonizing with the distant crashing waves. The moon cast an ethereal glow upon the water, illuminating the path ahead and revealing glimpses of its hidden secrets.

As Shannon moved forward, her senses heightened, capturing every sound and breath that echoed through the stillness of the night. The salty scent of the ocean mingled with the crisp nighttime air, filling her lungs with a sense of anticipation. The symphony of whispers and murmurs from unseen forces seemed to dance on her skin, leaving her both awe-inspired and apprehensive.

Her footsteps echoed against the wooden planks, their cadence guiding her deeper into the heart of Raymond's nocturnal surf sessions. With each step closer to her destination, Shannon's heartbeat quickened in rhythm with the crashing waves. There was an undeniable energy in the air—an invisible force that seemed to vibrate within her very being.

As she reached the end of the pier, Shannon's gaze fixated on the vast expanse of black water stretching out before her. The silver rays of moonlight danced upon its surface, creating an ethereal tapestry that merged with the ebb and flow of the ocean's rhythms. She couldn't help but be captivated by the mesmerizing beauty unfolding before her eyes.

The crashing waves against weathered pilings filled Shannon's ears, adding to the sense of timelessness and wonder that saturated the atmosphere. It was as if nature itself whispered ancient secrets, yearning for someone to unlock their mysteries. Shannon listened intently, hoping to discern whispers from hidden depths carried upon the gentle breeze.

With resolve burning bright within her, Shannon knelt down and studied the sand with fervor. Her fingertips delicately traced patterns in the fine grains, searching for any signs left behind by Raymond's nocturnal surf sessions. She combed through the darkness with a sense of purpose, her touch gentle yet purposeful, hoping to uncover any potential clues that may reveal themselves in this hidden landscape.

Suddenly, a glimmer caught Shannon's eye—a tattered surf-board partially buried in the sand a few feet away. Excitement surged within her as she rushed towards it, her flashlight casting a beam of light upon its weathered surface. The engraving etched into its wood made her heart skip a beat—"Seeker of Shadows." The words seemed to resonate with her own journey, carrying a weight of meaning that tantalized her curiosity.

In that moment, Shannon felt a deep connection to Ray-mond—an understanding that his fascination with surfing under moonlight held more significance than she could have ever imagined. It was as if this surfboard, with its inscription, held the key to unlocking the shadows that consumed his troubled mind.

With a racing heart, Shannon carefully jotted down the details in her notepad, her pen hovering over each word with intention. The revelation of the surfboard's inscription sparked a surge of determination within her—a resolve to dig deeper into the enigmatic world that surrounded Raymond's nocturnal surf sessions.

Continuing her exploration along the pier, Shannon's eyes scanned the surroundings for any other signs that might shed light on the mystery. She listened intently to the symphony of crashing waves and whistling wind, hoping to discern whispers of hidden secrets carried upon their haunting melodies.

As she moved closer to her destination, anticipation mingled with trepidation in Shannon's heart. The mysteries that en-veloped Raymond's fascination with surfing under moonlight seemed to pulse within her very veins. With each step, her connection to him deepened, forming an unbreakable bond that fueled her desire for answers.

The wind whispered through the pier's crevices, urging Shan-non onward. She adjusted the strap of her camera with a steady hand, ever ready to capture any evidence that might reveal itself in the night. This midnight venture held immeasurable potential—an encounter with an eerie presence, traces left behind by Raymond's enigmatic surf sessions, and perhaps even a glimpse into the depths of his troubled mind.

With determination etched upon her face, Shannon pressed on through the darkness—a solitary figure navigating through a labyrinth of shadows and secrets that awaited her. The night held its mysteries tightly, but she vowed to unveil them all.

Shannon stood at the edge of the Malibu Beach Pier, her footsteps muffled by the crashing waves. The moon's gentle glow cast an ethereal light upon the water below, illuminating the path ahead. With each breath, Shannon embraced the tranquility and anticipation that hung in the air.

Equipped with her camera, notepad, and flashlight, she ventured into the darkness, her resolve unwavering. The wooden planks creaked beneath her as she made her way towards the heart of the pier, their haunting echoes amplifying the silence of the night.

As she ventured deeper, her fiery red hair swaying in the cold ocean breeze, Shannon's senses were heightened. She absorbed every sound—the rhythmic crashing of waves against weathered pilings, the distant call of seagulls riding the nocturnal currents, and the whispered songs of the winds streaming through hidden crevices.

With each step forward, Shannon's anticipation grew. Her curiosity swelled alongside a burning desire for answers. Raymond's fascination with surfing under moonlight had led her to this desolate place, and now she aimed to uncover its secrets.

The wooden planks groaned beneath her as she reached the end of the pier. Gazing out into the vast expanse of black water, Shannon scanned the deserted beach below. The pale moonlight cast elongated shadows along the shoreline, making it difficult to discern any potential clues.

Undeterred, Shannon knelt down and carefully examined the sand. Her trained eyes searched for signs—footprints left behind by Raymond's nocturnal surf sessions or any belongings he might have left behind. As she combed through the darkness, her fingers tracing patterns in the fine grains, hope mingled with trepidation.

Suddenly, a glimmer caught Shannon's eye—a tattered surfboard half-buried in the sand a few feet away. Her heart raced with excitement as she rushed towards it and read an engraving that read "Seeker of Shadows," sparking a surge of excitement and a renewed determination to uncover the truth.

With the surfboard in hand, Shannon resumed her exploration along the pier. The sound of crashing waves filled her ears, adding to the mystical atmosphere that surrounded her.

The night air grew colder as Shannon ventured further into the darkness. Her footsteps echoed against the wooden planks, following her like whispers from unseen forces. She couldn't

39

help but feel a connection to Raymond's experiences—the allure and danger that lurked beneath the surface of this picturesque beach town.

With each passing moment, Shannon's curiosity deepened, driving her forward into uncharted territory. The mysteries that enveloped Raymond's nocturnal escapades became intertwined with her own journey—each step bringing her closer to the truth.

The wind whispered through the pier's crevices, urging Shannon onward. With a steady hand, she adjusted the strap of her camera and continued her meticulous search for clues. The night held its secrets tightly, but Shannon was determined to unravel them all.

She knew that this midnight venture held the potential to reveal more than she could have ever imagined—an encounter with an eerie presence, traces left behind by Raymond's enigmatic surfing sessions, and perhaps even a glimpse into the depths of his troubled mind.

With resolute steps, Shannon pressed on through the darkness, guided by a mix of anticipation, apprehension, and an insatiable curiosity. She had embarked on a journey that would challenge her perception of reality and test her resolve. The night held its secrets, and it was up to Shannon to unveil them all.

As she moved further along the pier, shadows danced around her—whispering secrets she strained to hear. The sound of crashing waves grew louder, filling the air with a symphony of rhythm and mystery. In this enchanting darkness, Shannon felt a surge of excitement—an invitation into a world where the surreal melded with reality.

The moon's glow reflected off the water, creating an other-worldly shimmer. Shannon's gaze fixed upon the horizon, searching for any sign of Raymond and his nocturnal surf sessions. But the beach remained deserted, its secrets buried beneath layers of sand and time.

Undeterred, Shannon pressed on, her steps quickening with each passing moment. She knew that answers lay hidden within these shadows—answers that would unlock the mystery of Raymond's fascination with surfing under moonlight.

As she approached the end of the pier, Shannon's heart quickened with a mix of anticipation and trepidation. The crashing waves grew louder, their rhythmic symphony echoing through her every fiber. And then she saw it—a figure rising from the water with ethereal grace.

Shannon's breath caught in her throat as she watched the figure ride a massive wave, their body merging seamlessly with the ocean's power. The moon cast an otherworldly glow upon them, revealing their features for a fleeting moment—eyes filled with sadness and a deep understanding of Raymond's torment.

In that instant, Shannon felt a connection—a bond that tran-scended time and space. She sensed that this figure held the key to unlocking Raymond's secrets, the truth behind his obsession with surfing under moonlight.

But as quickly as they appeared, the figure vanished back into the darkness, leaving Shannon standing alone on the pier—bewildered yet filled with a newfound sense of purpose. She knew that she couldn't turn back now—the enigmatic presence had revealed itself, igniting a flame within her that refused to be extinguished.

With resolute determination, Shannon continued her exploration along the pier, her footsteps echoing against the wooden planks. Each sound seemed to reverberate through the stillness—a reminder of the mysteries yet to be unraveled.

As she retraced her steps, Shannon searched for any physical evidence left behind by the figure—a trace of their existence, a tangible clue that would lead her closer to the truth. But the pier stood silent and empty, its secrets buried beneath layers of history.

Frustration threatened to consume Shannon, but she refused to give in. The night still held its mysteries tightly, but she knew that time was on her side. Guided by a newfound determination, she pressed on—each step affirming her commitment to unlock the enigma of Raymond's fascination with surfing under moonlight.

The wind whispered through the pier's crevices, urging Shannon onward. The crashing waves seemed to echo her determination—a resounding symphony of possibilities. She adjusted the strap of her camera with steady hands, ready to capture any evidence that might reveal itself in the night.

This midnight venture had become more than a quest for answers—it had become a journey of self-discovery. With every step forward, Shannon delved deeper into her own soul, unraveling the layers of mystery that shrouded her own desires and fears.

As the moon bathed the pier in silver light, Shannon was filled with an undeniable sense of purpose—a conviction that she would uncover the truth no matter what obstacles lay ahead. The enigmatic secrets of Raymond's nocturnal surf sessions called out to her, and she vowed to follow their siren's call until their secrets were revealed.

With renewed determination and unwavering resolve, Shannon pressed on—into the darkness, into the shadows that held the key to Raymond's troubled mind. The night held its secrets tightly, but she was determined to unveil them all.

7

Cryptic Messages: Unraveling the Silver Siren

Shannon cautiously followed the anonymous tip that led her to a secluded beach known for its mystical aura. The moon's gentle glow cast an ethereal light upon the dark sand, creating an atmosphere of mystery and anticipation. As she traversed the desolate beach, the crashing waves provided a haunting melody, heightening the suspense that coursed through her veins.

Every step Shannon took seemed to be guided by an unseen force, as if the very air whispered ancient secrets. The silver rays of moonlight danced upon the water, revealing glimpses of hidden depths and setting the stage for an eerie encounter. Her senses were heightened, attuned to every sound and breath that echoed through the stillness of the night.

As Shannon ventured deeper into the darkness, she could feel an unexplainable presence watching her every move. It was as if unseen eyes followed her, their gaze filled with curiosity and skepticism. The sound of crashing waves grew louder, serving as a reminder of the mysteries yet to be unraveled.

Particularly drawn to a hidden cave nestled within the jagged cliffs, Shannon felt a pull towards its entrance. Covered in ancient symbols and markings, it exuded an enigmatic energy that beckoned her forward. Each step brought her closer to uncovering the secrets hidden within its depths.

The air grew heavier with each passing moment, as if the cave itself held its breath in anticipation of what was to come. Shannon approached with caution but determination, ready to confront whatever awaited her inside. Its darkness seemed to swallow any semblance of light, adding to the sense of foreboding that saturated the atmosphere.

The rocky ground beneath Shannon's feet gave way to a carpet of soft sand as she entered the cave. The sound of her footsteps echoed in the confined space, intertwining with the hushed whispers carried on the air. She shone her flashlight upon the walls, illuminating intricate symbols etched into the rock—the ancient language of this mysterious place.

With each passing moment, Shannon's heart pounded in her chest, mirroring the intensity of her pursuit. She studied the symbols, their meaning just beyond her grasp. As she traced her fingers along their lines, a jolt of recognition coursed through her—a flash of memory long forgotten.

In that moment, Shannon felt an inexplicable connection to the cave—an unspoken link between her past and present. The enigma of the silver siren weighed heavily upon her mind as she delved deeper into this hidden realm. She knew that deciphering these symbols held the key to unlocking Raymond's secrets, but they also opened doors to her own self-discovery.

As she moved further into the depths of the cave, Shannon's excitement mingled with trepidation. The air grew colder, chilling her to the bone. Shadows danced on the walls as if alive, whispering secrets only she could hear. Every sense was heightened—every sound, every scent, every touch—leading her closer to the truth.

Suddenly, a faint glow caught Shannon's attention—a flickering light emanating from a small crevice in the cave wall. Her curiosity piqued, she approached it cautiously, wary of what lay beyond. With bated breath, she peered inside and gasped at what she found.

The crevice opened into a hidden chamber bathed in an ethereal glow. The light seemed to emanate from a single source—a mystical artifact perched upon a pedestal in the center of the room. Shannon stepped forward, entranced by its beauty and drawn to its power.

As she reached out to touch the artifact, a surge of energy coursed through her body. Images flooded her mind—visions of Raymond, waves crashing around him as he rode his surfboard under moonlit skies. The silver siren materialized before her eyes—a spectral figure guiding Raymond through his nocturnal journeys.

In that moment, Shannon understood the significance of the silver siren—an ancient creature woven into the fabric of Malibu's history. This mysterious being held sway over Raymond's mind and soul, its allure and danger entwined with his every thought. The artifact on the pedestal was a gateway to uncovering its secrets—a catalyst for Shannon's quest for truth.

With newfound determination, Shannon pledged to delve deeper into Raymond's connection with the silver siren. She ran her fingers along the artifact's smooth surface, feeling a sense of purpose surge through her veins. The enigmatic presence that had guided her to this cave now banded them together, intertwining their fates in a tapestry of mystery and revelation.

As she ventured further into this hidden world, Shannon knew she had only scratched the surface of the truth. The cave whispered its secrets, urging her onward in her quest to unravel the enigma of the silver siren and bring Raymond's torment to light.

And so, armed with newfound knowledge and resolve, Shannon left the hidden chamber behind, ready to face the challenges that lay ahead. The moonlight embraced her as she stepped back onto the desolate beach—her feet sinking into the soft sand, marking each step towards an uncertain future.

Little did she know that this eerie encounter was only the beginning—a glimpse into a world brimming with mystery, secrets, and the power of hallucinations. The silver siren's embrace would lead Shannon on a thrilling investigation through the tangled web of Malibu's past and present—an exploration that offered both healing and self-discovery.

8

Broken Reflections

Shannon sat restlessly in the therapist's office, her anticipation mounting as she awaited the start of her session with Dr. Marissa Lawson. The room exuded a calm and serene energy, from the soft lighting to the soothing artwork that adorned the walls. Shannon took in the comforting scents of lavender and eucalyptus, allowing herself to be enveloped in the therapeutic ambiance.

As Dr. Lawson entered the room, she greeted Shannon with a warm smile, her voice carrying a gentle yet confident tone. "Good morning, Shannon," she said calmly. "How are you feeling today?"

Shannon shifted in her seat, feeling a mix of nervousness and determination coursing through her veins. "I'm anxious, but also ready to face whatever comes," she replied, her voice laced with emotion.

Dr. Lawson nodded understandingly, taking a seat across from

Shannon on the plush couch. "I admire your courage," she said softly. "Today, we're going to delve into some deep-rooted traumas in order to gain insight into Raymond's experiences. Are you prepared for what may arise?"

Shannon took a deep breath, steeling herself for the emotional journey ahead. "I'm as prepared as I can be," she answered truthfully. "I want to understand Raymond's struggles and empathize with his journey."

Dr. Lawson nodded again, her eyes filled with compassion. "I appreciate your commitment to this process," she said sincerely. "Now, let us begin by engaging in some deep breathing exercises. Close your eyes and focus on your breath."

Shannon obeyed, closing her eyes and inhaling deeply. With each breath, she felt a sense of calm washing over her, grounding her in the present moment.

"Now, I want you to visualize a peaceful place," Dr. Lawson instructed gently. "Somewhere that brings you comfort and safety."

In Shannon's mind, a vivid image of a serene beach materialized. The sound of crashing waves and the feel of warm sand beneath her feet filled her senses. She felt a deep sense of peace as she immersed herself in this tranquil setting.

Dr. Lawson's voice broke through Shannon's reverie. "Now, Shannon, I want you to think about a specific traumatic event from your past," she said softly. "Focus on the emotions that arise and allow them to surface."

Shannon's breath hitched slightly as she brought to mind the painful memory of being betrayed by a close friend. The raw emotions swelled within her chest, threatening to overwhelm her.

"Take your time," Dr. Lawson encouraged gently. "Allow the emotions to come, but remember that you are safe here with me."

As Shannon let herself fully experience the pain and betrayal of the memory, tears spilled down her cheeks. She felt an immense release, a weight lifting from her shoulders as she acknowledged the depth of her own pain.

After what felt like an eternity, Shannon opened her eyes and met Dr. Lawson's gaze. "That was intense," she admitted, her voice trembling with vulnerability.

Dr. Lawson nodded in understanding. "Sometimes, revisiting our traumas can be both painful and healing," she said. "It's important to honor those emotions and give yourself permission to heal."

Shannon wiped away her tears, a newfound determination shining in her eyes. "I understand now," she said with conviction. "By confronting my own traumas, I can gain a deeper understanding of Raymond's experiences and his journey towards healing."

Dr. Lawson smiled warmly, touching Shannon's hand lightly. "You've taken an important step today," she said softly. "Remember that healing is not linear, but it is possible."

As Shannon left Dr. Lawson's office that day, she carried with her a renewed sense of purpose. The emotions she had confronted were still raw, but now they fueled her drive to unlock the truth behind Raymond's shattered memory.

With each step she took, Shannon knew that she was one step closer to unraveling the enigma of psilocybin therapy and discovering the secrets that lay hidden within Raymond's fragmented mind. Armed with her own healing process as a guiding light, she was more determined than ever to bring justice and closure to her former classmate. The next chapter of her investigation awaited, and Shannon embarked on this treacherous journey with a newfound resilience and an unwavering commitment to unveiling the truth.

9

Surfing the Shadows

Shannon and Blaise woke before dawn, their excitement palpable as they prepared for a day of surfing at a secluded spot known for its powerful and challenging breaks. The crisp morning air carried a salty tang that invigorated their senses, heightening their anticipation.

With their surfboards tucked securely under their arms, Shannon and Blaise made their way to the beach. The crashing waves beckoned them with their rhythmic roar, the energy in the air electrifying. Each step brought them closer to the water, their hearts pounding in sync with the sound of the crashing surf.

As they reached the shoreline, the sun began to rise over the horizon, casting a warm golden glow across the ocean. The water shimmered with promise, inviting them to paddle out and ride the morning swell.

Positioning themselves on their boards, Shannon and Blaise began to paddle. The cool water splashed against their faces as they navigated through the breaking waves, each stroke bringing them closer to the lineup.

A sense of serenity washed over Shannon as she floated on her board, waiting for the perfect wave. She breathed in deeply, taking in the salty air and allowing herself to fully embrace the moment. There was no other place she'd rather be than here, in Mother Nature's playground.

Blaise's face lit up as he spotted a promising set rolling in. He turned to Shannon, an eager glint in his eyes. "This is it," he exclaimed, his voice filled with anticipation.

They both paddled furiously, matching each other's pace, striving to catch this wave together. As they felt the swell lift their boards, they effortlessly hopped onto their feet, riding the face of the wave with grace and determination.

The world around them became a blur as they carved through the mesmerizing blue wall of water. Shannon could feel the power of the wave beneath her feet, propelling her forward with exhilarating force. It was a dance with the elements, a harmonious partnership between human and nature.

As they rode the wave towards the shore, Shannon couldn't help but smile. This was what freedom felt like – the rush of adrenaline, the pure joy of being in sync with the ocean's rhythm. In that moment, she felt alive and connected to something greater than herself.

The ride came to an end, and Shannon and Blaise paddled back out, eager for another exhilarating experience. They spent the morning chasing waves, their laughter filling the air as they shared the sheer thrill of riding nature's untamed power.

With each wave they caught, their bond grew stronger. They were more than just friends now; they were partners in this quest for truth, united by their shared determination to unravel Raymond's secrets.

As the sun climbed higher in the sky, casting its warm glow over the beach, Shannon felt a sense of fulfillment wash over her. She was exactly where she needed to be – immersed in nature's embrace, surfing alongside a friend who understood her deepest desires.

Little did she know that this day of chasing waves would lead them further down the path of discovery. Each swell carried with it a clue, a glimpse into Raymond's world before his disappearance. And with each ride, Shannon grew more determined to find answers, no matter where the waves may take her.

Shannon and Blaise emerged from the water, their bodies glistening with droplets of saltwater. The exhilaration of riding the morning's waves still coursed through their veins, fueling their spirits as they made their way back to Blaise's beachfront apartment.

Inside, the walls were adorned with faded photographs of surfers caught in mid-air, frozen moments of triumph captured on film. Shannon and Blaise settled onto the worn-out couch, their bodies sinking into the comfort of its familiar embrace.

With Raymond's surf journal open in front of them, they began to delve into its pages, searching for clues that could shed light on his experiences and his ultimate disappearance. Each entry held a fragment of Raymond's soul, a piece of his journey that had been left behind.

As Shannon read aloud Raymond's musings about the taste of salt on his lips and the thrill of catching the perfect wave, a sense of admiration and understanding filled the room. It was as if she could hear Raymond's voice echoing through the words, his love for surfing infusing every line.

Blaise leaned forward, pointing to a particular passage in the journal. "Listen to this," he exclaimed, excitement evident in his voice. "Raymond writes about 'the silver siren' calling to him from beneath the waves."

A shiver ran down Shannon's spine as she absorbed the words. The mention of the silver siren struck a chord within her, igniting a spark of curiosity and urgency. It was a thread that connected their investigation to something deeper, something more mysterious than they could have imagined.

Their eyes met, gleaming with a shared determination. The pieces were slowly aligning, leading them closer to understanding Raymond's world before he vanished without a trace.

As they continued flipping through the journal, they discovered references to specific locations and dates that coincided with

Raymond's last known whereabouts. The words on those pages became bread crumbs, guiding their way through the labyrinth of his experiences.

Closing the surf journal, Shannon clutched it tightly to her chest, feeling a surge of purpose pulsate within her. "We have to follow Raymond's footprints," she declared, her voice filled with conviction. "These locations mentioned here—they hold the key to unraveling the mystery of his disappearance."

Blaise nodded in agreement, his gaze steady. "I'm with you all the way," he affirmed, his loyalty unwavering. "Together, we'll chase down these secrets and bring Raymond's truth into the light."

The setting sun cast long shadows across the room, its warm golden light painting their faces with a sense of determination. As they made plans for their next move, Shannon felt a renewed sense of purpose coursing through her veins.

With each location they would visit, each piece of Raymond's story they would uncover, they were one step closer to solving the enigma that had consumed their lives. The invisible ties that bound them to Raymond grew stronger with every passing moment, propelling them forward on their shared quest.

As they stepped out into the fading light of day, Shannon and Blaise carried with them the weight of responsibility and the unwavering desire for truth. The journey ahead might be treacherous and unpredictable, but their bond was unbreakable.

With Raymond's surf journal as their guide, they embarked on this new chapter of their investigation. The possibilities stretched out before them like an infinite wave, waiting to carry them closer to the truth they so desperately sought.

The chase continued, waves crashing against their determination as they delved deeper into the secrets hidden beneath the surface. Through shadows and uncertainty, they would forge a path towards resolution, unraveling the enigma of Raymond's disappearance—one untamed wave at a time.

10

Melodies of Remembrance

Shannon sat cross-legged on the floor of her apartment, her attention fixed on the old shoe box in front of her. Dust particles floated in the air as she carefully lifted the lid, revealing a collection of forgotten treasures. Amongst the trinkets and mementos, her eyes fell upon a mix tape labeled "Heartbeat City."

Intrigued by its significance, Shannon held the cassette tape delicately in her hands, feeling the weight of the past within its plastic casing. She had stumbled upon Raymond's surf journal, unlocking fragments of his mind through his writings. Now, this mix tape seemed like another key to understanding his mysterious disappearance.

With a mix of anticipation and curiosity, Shannon inserted the tape into an old cassette player she had dusted off just for this occasion. The whirring sound of the tape being wound up filled the room, adding to the sense of nostalgia that hung in the air.

As the music began to play, Shannon closed her eyes and allowed herself to be transported into Raymond's world. Each song served as a portal to his memories, evoking emotions and moments long forgotten. From the sunny melodies that captured carefree summer days to the haunting lyrics that delved into life's deeper questions, Shannon felt connected to Raymond on a profound level.

The songs carried whispers of joy, longing, and introspection. They painted a vivid picture of Raymond's state of mind before he vanished without a trace. Shannon could almost visualize him driving along coastal roads, with the music blaring from his car speakers and wind rushing through open windows.

One track stood out among the rest—a melancholic ballad that spoke directly to her soul. Its haunting melody echoed through her being, stirring emotions she couldn't quite name. It was as if Raymond's essence was seeping into her consciousness, leaving an indelible mark on her own journey.

The mix tape became a time machine, transporting Shannon to Raymond's moments of reflection and revelation. The lyrics hinted at a deeper understanding of the world, and as Shannon listened intently, she began to decipher the hidden meanings within each song.

The music whispered secrets and unveiled emotions that had remained dormant within Raymond. It was a revelation, a glimpse into the inner workings of his mind. Shannon felt an unbreakable bond forming between them, bridging the gap between past and present.

As the final song faded away, Shannon opened her eyes, a mix of wonder and determination sparkling in their depths. She knew that this mix tape held the key to unlocking the mystery surrounding Raymond's disappearance. The music had become their guide, leading her closer to the truth.

With each note and lyric etched into her memory, Shannon made a silent promise to follow Raymond's musical footprints. She would dive deep into the lyrics, explore their hidden meanings, and embark on a journey that would unravel the enigma of his vanishing.

As she carefully removed the tape from the cassette player, Shannon knew that she had stumbled upon something extraordinary. The mix tape "Heartbeat City" had become more than just a collection of songs—it was a window into Raymond's soul.

Armed with this newfound knowledge and fueled by a thirst for answers, Shannon closed her fingers around the mix tape, ready to chase down the secrets it held. She could feel the energy building within her, propelling her forward on this exhilarating investigation in search of truth and closure.

As she tucked the mix tape safely back into its shoe box resting place, Shannon made a vow to herself. She would follow Raymond's musical cues and uncover any hidden messages embedded in "Heartbeat City." With each lyric dissected and each chord analyzed, she hoped to unravel the enigma of his disappearance one melodic strand at a time.

Leaving her apartment filled with anticipation, Shannon embarked on a new chapter of her investigation. She would delve deeper into the music, seeking connections and meanings that could shed light on Raymond's world before he disappeared. Armed with the power of "Heartbeat City," she was ready to face any challenge that lay ahead.

As Shannon stepped out into the bustling city streets, the sounds of everyday life melded with the echoes of Raymond's music in her mind. The lyrics became a constant companion, guiding her steps and fueling her determination.

The mysteries of "Heartbeat City" beckoned to her, promising an enlightening journey. And as Shannon set off on this new adventure, she knew that the enigma of Raymond's disappearance was within her grasp—just waiting to be unraveled, one melodic note at a time.

11

The Whispering Shores

Shannon stepped off the bus, her heart pounding with a mix of excitement and trepidation as she arrived in the small coastal town known for its alternative healing practices. The sun warmed her skin, and a sense of tranquility washed over her. This was the place where she hoped to find answers - a rumored expert in psilocybin therapy who might shed light on Raymond's experiences.

As Shannon walked through the streets lined with charming boutiques and quaint cafes, she couldn't help but feel a certain energy in the air. It was as if the town itself held secrets waiting to be discovered. She entered a local café that seemed to emit an irresistible aroma of freshly brewed coffee. Soft jazz played in the background, mingling with hushed conversations.

Approaching the counter, Shannon caught snippets of whispers about the elusive therapist she sought. Mysterious tales of healing and transformation circulated among the patrons, piquing her curiosity even more. This was the place where connections were made, where secrets were exchanged.

The café owner, a warm smile lighting up their face, sensed Shannon's intrigue. They leaned across the counter, their voice barely above a whisper, and told her about the rumored expert in psilocybin therapy. Their words spoke of a reclusive figure known for unconventional methods and a profound understanding of the human mind.

Undeterred by the owner's skepticism about the therapist's willingness to share information, Shannon remained determined. Raymond's disappearance weighed heavily on her heart, propelling her forward in her quest for truth.

With newfound resolve, Shannon set off on a search for the therapist's office. The cobblestone streets guided her through the picturesque town, each step bringing her closer to her destination. Vibrant colors adorned the buildings, creating a captivating atmosphere filled with warmth and charm.

Her footsteps eventually led her to a secluded area tucked away among towering trees. A sense of tranquility settled upon her as she caught sight of the therapist's office nestled within the lush greenery. It seemed to exist in harmony with nature, its presence both soothing and secretive.

Approaching the office door, Shannon's heart thumped with anticipation. She hesitated for a moment, taking in the sights and sounds around her. The rustling of leaves in the gentle breeze seemed to whisper encouragement, urging her to knock and enter.

Summoning her courage, Shannon rapped lightly on the door. It swung open just enough for her to slip inside, revealing a world filled with soft lighting and ethereal artwork. The room exuded serenity, inviting Shannon to step further into its embrace.

Behind a desk adorned with ancient texts and healing crystals sat Dr. Avery Sinclair, the renowned expert in psilocybin therapy. Their presence commanded attention, their piercing gaze reflecting a depth of knowledge that seemed almost other-worldly. A sense of calm radiated from them, drawing Shannon deeper into their realm.

As they engaged in conversation, Shannon found herself captivated by Dr. Sinclair's gentle yet confident demeanor. Their voice washed over her like a soothing balm, offering insight into the nature of psilocybin therapy and its potential effects on the mind and soul.

Dr. Sinclair revealed their unorthodox approach, rooted in ancient rituals and a deep connection to nature. They spoke of how psilocybin had the power to unlock hidden truths within one's psyche, but also warned of the dangers that lay within its realm if approached without proper guidance.

Suspense hung in the air as Dr. Sinclair shared disturbing anecdotes about individuals who had undergone psilocybin therapy without supervision, resulting in severe psychological trauma. Shadows danced across the room, casting an eerie ambience that played with Shannon's perception of reality.

Torn between her unwavering determination and concern for the potential risks involved, Shannon grappled with internal conflict. The dimly lit room mirrored the uncertainty that welled up inside her, leaving her questioning the choices she had made in her quest for answers.

But Shannon's relentless pursuit of the truth pushed her forward. She tentatively agreed to undergo a supervised psilocybin session with Dr. Sinclair, embracing the unknown in her search for Raymond's experiences. The gravity of the moment settled upon her as she prepared herself mentally and emotionally for the transformative journey that lay ahead.

The room was filled with an air of anticipation and mystery as Shannon sat in the plush armchair, waiting for the session to begin. The flickering candle on the desk cast shifting shadows across the room, heightening her senses. In this moment, she knew that she was about to embark on a profound exploration of her own mind.

Dr. Sinclair approached Shannon, their eyes filled with empathy and understanding. "Are you ready?" they asked softly.

Taking a deep breath, Shannon nodded. She was ready to confront the depths of her subconscious, to uncover the hidden truths that lay within and find the answers she so desperately sought.

With gentle guidance from Dr. Sinclair, Shannon consumed the contents of the vial containing a carefully measured dose of psilocybin. The bitter taste lingered on her tongue, but it was merely a prelude to the journey that awaited her.

As the effects of the psilocybin began to take hold, Shannon closed her eyes and surrendered herself to the unknown. Colors danced behind her eyelids, patterns formed and dissolved, and a sense of interconnectedness enveloped her consciousness.

Memories flooded back like waves crashing on a shore, each one carrying a piece of Raymond's story. The visions swirled together, fragments of his life merging with hopes and fears of her own. Emotions rose and fell like tides, crashing against the shores of her heart.

Time lost meaning as Shannon traversed landscapes of the mind, both familiar and uncharted. She waded through memories and emotions, piecing together the puzzle that was Raymond's disappearance.

In moments of clarity, Shannon found herself standing on a desolate beach, the crashing waves echoing the turmoil in her heart. The sun dipped below the horizon, casting long shadows that danced along the sand. In that lonely moment, she found solace in the beauty of the unknown, realizing that some truths are meant to remain elusive.

As the psilocybin journey came to an end, Shannon opened her eyes, her mind flooded with a profound sense of connection to Raymond and a renewed understanding of her own purpose. Dr. Sinclair's reassuring presence brought her back to reality, their gentle smile conveying a shared understanding of the transformative power of this experience.

The room bathed in soft light seemed to exhale with Shannon as she took a deep breath and allowed herself to ground in the present moment. The mysteries surrounding Raymond's disappearance remained, but she had been granted a glimpse into his world and a deeper understanding of her own self.

As she left the office, Shannon carried with her a sense of profound grace and gratitude for the journey she had embarked upon. The answers she sought were still elusive, but she now possessed a newfound strength and clarity to face the enigma head-on.

The coastal town whispered its secrets as Shannon walked through its streets once more. The cafés exuded warmth, inviting her to linger and reflect on the revelations from her psilocybin journey. She knew that the path ahead would be challenging, but armed with this newfound perspective, she felt ready to continue unraveling the silver siren's secrets that had haunted her for so long.

With each step forward, Shannon embraced the uncertainty and mystery that lay ahead. The healing possibilities within the realm of psilocybin therapy illuminated her path, offering a fresh perspective on healing and self-discovery.

As the sun began to set over the town, Shannon found solace in the knowledge that she was not alone in her pursuit of truth. The echoes of Raymond's experiences reverberated within her,

67

propelling her forward on this thrilling investigation that would forever change her life.

12

Unmasking the Enigma: Shannon unravels the mystery behind the silver siren and confronts her about her involvement in Raymond's vanishing.

Peering Behind the Curtain

Shannon's heart raced with anticipation as she stood outside the unassuming entrance of the hidden underground club. Its location in a dimly lit alleyway lent an air of mystery and enchantment to the venue. She couldn't help but feel a shiver of excitement as she stepped inside, her senses immediately captivated by the sights and sounds that surrounded her.

The bouncer eyed Shannon suspiciously as she attempted to blend into the crowd. She had taken great care to disguise herself, wearing a wig and sunglasses to conceal her identity. With a deep breath, she convinced herself that this was the only way to get closer to the truth, to peel back the layers of deception surrounding the silver siren and her connection to Raymond's disappearance.

As Shannon made her way through a maze-like corridor, vibrant neon lights bathed the walls in an array of colors, creating a disorienting effect. Hypnotic music pulsed through the air, reverberating in her chest. It was as if she had stepped into another dimension, a realm where reality blurred and fantasies took form.

The performers she encountered along the way wore elaborate costumes and masks, each one more intricate than the last. They moved with grace and precision, their movements synchronized in a mesmerizing display that left Shannon both awestruck and unsettled. Their eyes conveyed a sense of mystery, drawing her deeper into their enigmatic world.

As Shannon emerged from the labyrinthine corridor, she found herself in a dimly lit room packed with eager spectators. The atmosphere was heavy with anticipation, a palpable tension that hung in the air like an invisible veil. The stage glimmered with intricate props and billowing fog, casting an ethereal glow over the room.

The silver siren took center stage, her mere presence commanding attention. She wore a flowing gown that shimmered under the spotlight, accentuating every graceful movement she made. As the music swelled, she began to dance, her body moving with a fluidity that seemed almost supernatural.

Shannon's eyes were fixed on the silver siren, her heart pounding in her chest. There was something undeniably captivating about the way the siren moved, as if she possessed an otherworldly aura that drew everyone in attendance into her spell. The room fell silent, each spectator holding their breath, entranced by the performance unfolding before them.

As the silver siren twirled and glided across the stage, Shannon felt a sense of familiarity begin to stir within her. The movements, the symbolism conveyed through her dance — they evoked memories and emotions that had long been buried deep within Shannon's subconscious. It was as if the silver siren held the key to unlocking the enigma surrounding Raymond's disappearance.

The atmosphere in the room grew increasingly charged with each passing moment. A sense of unease settled over Shannon as she watched the silver siren's hypnotic performance unfold. Shadows danced along the walls, casting an eerie ambience that mirrored Shannon's growing apprehension. Something about this spectacle felt deeply unsettling, as if the answers she sought were just beyond her grasp.

As the performance reached its climax, Shannon caught a glimpse of familiar eyes beneath the silver siren's veil. Her breath caught in her throat as a sudden realization struck her like a bolt of lightning. The pieces of the puzzle began to align in her mind, forming a picture that both frightened and exhilarated her.

In that moment, Shannon knew that she had come face to face with the illusionist herself — the silver siren who held the secrets of Raymond's disappearance. And now, it was time for

71

Shannon to confront her, to demand answers and unveil the truth hidden beneath the enchanting facade.

With determination burning in her eyes, Shannon waited backstage for the silver siren to emerge from the stage. She knew that this confrontation would change everything, that the illusion would be shattered and the truth laid bare. The air crackled with anticipation as she prepared to peer behind the curtain and reveal the silver siren's true identity.

As the final notes of the music faded away, the silver siren gracefully stepped off the stage and into the backstage area. Shannon's heart raced as she approached, her voice steady but filled with urgency.

"Jacki," Shannon said, her voice just above a whisper. "I know who you are."

The silver siren turned to face her, a mix of surprise and uncertainty flashing across her face. For a moment, Jacki's eyes met Shannon's, their intensity mirroring the tension that hung between them.

"You have no idea what you're talking about," Jacki replied, her voice tinged with a hint of defiance.

But Shannon was undeterred. She had spent countless hours piecing together the puzzle, following leads and uncovering connections that had led her to this very moment. The truth was finally within reach, and she wasn't about to let it slip away.

"Raymond disappeared after he became involved with you," Shannon pressed on, her voice filled with conviction. "You can't hide from the truth any longer."

A flicker of emotion crossed Jacki's face, but it was quickly replaced by a cold indifference. She took a step closer to Shannon, their eyes locked in an intense stare-down.

"You think you know everything," Jacki sneered. "But you're just a naive outsider stumbling into a world you know nothing about."

Shannon squared her shoulders, refusing to back down. She had come too far to be intimidated by Jacki's attempts to deflect and undermine her. She had seen through the illusions and now it was time for the reckoning.

"I may not have all the answers yet," Shannon admitted. "But I won't stop until I uncover the truth. And you can be sure that I won't let you get away with whatever you've done."

Tension hung heavy in the air as Shannon and Jacki stood at a crossroads, each one determined to protect their own interests. The room seemed to hold its breath, waiting for the confrontation to reach its climax.

But before the standoff could escalate any further, a voice cut through the tension from behind them.

"What's going on here?"

Both Shannon and Jacki turned to see a figure emerging from the shadows. It was Dr. Avery Sinclair, the renowned expert in psilocybin therapy. Their presence added another layer of intrigue to the already charged atmosphere.

"I thought it might be you, Shannon," Dr. Sinclair said, their voice calm but tinged with curiosity. "I've been following your investigation closely. You're treading into dangerous territory."

Shannon's mind raced as she tried to process this unexpected turn of events. What was Dr. Sinclair doing here, and what did they know about Jacki's involvement in Raymond's disappearance?

"You have a choice to make, Shannon," Dr. Sinclair continued, their gaze unwavering. "Do you want the truth, no matter the cost? Or will you walk away and leave this mystery unsolved?"

The weight of Dr. Sinclair's words settled upon Shannon's shoulders. She had come too far to turn back now, to allow fear or uncertainty to dictate her actions. This was her chance to finally uncover the secrets that had haunted her for so long.

"I choose truth," Shannon declared, her voice strong and resolute.

The room seemed to exhale as Shannon made her choice. The path ahead would undoubtedly be treacherous, but she was ready to face whatever challenges awaited her. With Dr. Sinclair by her side, she knew that she had an ally in this journey.

As Shannon and Dr. Sinclair prepared to delve deeper into the enigma surrounding Raymond's disappearance, the stage was set for a confrontation that would unveil secrets that had long been hidden in the shadows. The truth awaited, shrouded in uncertainty and danger, but Shannon was ready to embrace the unknown, no matter the cost.

13

A Descent into Madness: Raymond's mental health spirals as hallucinations consume him, blurring the line between reality and delusion.

Scene 1: A Descent into Madness

Raymond's mind was a tumultuous storm of twisted thoughts and distorted perceptions. As his hallucinations grew more vivid, reality and fantasy merged into an enigmatic dance. Shadows danced in the corners of his vision, taunting him with their elusive forms. Whispers echoed through his mind, like murmurs from the darkest recesses of his soul.

Part 1: Raymond's hallucinations become more intense and vivid, blurring the boundary between his inner demons and the outside world. He sees shimmering figures in the shadows and hears haunting whispers that echo through his mind.

In the depths of the night, as darkness draped over Malibu

like a cloak, Raymond found himself lost in the maze of his own thoughts. Every flicker of movement in the periphery of his vision sent shivers down his spine. Figures, ethereal and shimmering, seemed to materialize before him before evaporating into nothingness. Their faces were familiar, yet their features distorted and grotesque, mirroring Raymond's deepest fears.

Part 2: His paranoia intensifies, convinced that the silver siren holds the key to his salvation. He becomes increasingly obsessed with finding her, believing that she alone can bring him peace and redemption.

As the hallucinations multiplied, so did Raymond's conviction that the silver siren held the answers to his tortured existence. She was an enigma, a mysterious figure whose allure both fascinated and terrified him. Raymond saw her face in every crowd, heard her melodic voice in each gust of wind. There was no escaping her presence, even in the recesses of his own fractured psyche.

Driven by an insatiable obsession, Raymond scoured the streets of Malibu in search of the silver siren's hiding place. Day after day, he wandered aimlessly, driven by an irrational faith that she alone could offer him salvation from the madness that consumed him. Others watched from a distance, unable to penetrate the fortress of paranoia that enveloped Raymond's fragile mind.

Part 3: Conflict arises as Raymond's actions become increasingly erratic and dangerous. He isolates himself from those around him, cutting ties with loved ones who try to intervene. His desperate quest for the silver siren puts not only himself but also others at risk.

As Raymond delved deeper into his obsession, he became a shadow of his former self. Those who cared for him were met with cold indifference or outright hostility. Friends and family pleaded for him to seek help, to break free from the clutches of his delusions, but their words fell on deaf ears.

Isolation was Raymond's only refuge. He shut himself away in the solitude of his apartment, cutting off all contact with the outside world. The walls echoed with his anguished cries, the only company he sought in the depths of despair.

But even in his seclusion, Raymond's actions sent ripples of concern through those who remained by his side. They saw the desperation etched into his eyes, the unraveling of sanity inching closer with each passing day. Fear mingled with sorrow as they understood that Raymond's relentless pursuit of the silver siren would ultimately lead him down a treacherous path.

Raymond stood at the precipice, teetering between reality and delusion. His mind had become a labyrinth of twisted thoughts and fragmented memories. With each step he took into the depths of his hallucinatory world, he pushed himself closer to the edge of self-destruction.

The descent into madness offered no solace, no respite from the torment within. It was a journey marked by confusion, fear, and an insatiable thirst for answers. And as Raymond ventured further into the abyss, Shannon and Blaise plotted their own course through the chaos, ready to face the consequences of their intertwined fates.

Lost in the Labyrinth

Raymond's surroundings blurred as he stumbled deeper into the labyrinthine forest. The dense foliage enveloped him, obscuring his vision and distorting reality. Every step felt uncertain, his footing unsteady on the uneven terrain. His heart raced as he pressed forward, guided by his delusions and a desperate desire to uncover the truth about the silver siren.

The forest seemed to stretch endlessly before him, its towering trees casting long shadows that danced across his path. Rays of sunlight filtered through the thick canopy above, illuminating patches of vibrant green moss and tangled underbrush. The air was thick with the scent of damp earth and decaying leaves, adding to the otherworldly atmosphere that surrounded him.

As Raymond navigated through the labyrinth of trees, their branches seemed to reach out like gnarled fingers, threatening to ensnare him in their clutches. The path ahead twisted and turned without rhyme or reason, leaving him disoriented and unsure of which direction to take. His mind teetered on the edge of clarity and chaos, mirroring the tangled undergrowth that seemed to mirror his fractured psyche.

With each passing moment, the forest grew darker and more foreboding. Shadows deepened, concealing unseen dangers lurking beyond Raymond's line of sight. Whispering echoes filled the air, their unintelligible words taunting him from all directions.

False paths appeared amidst the dense undergrowth, leading Raymond astray and deepening his sense of disorientation. He would follow what seemed like a promising route, only to find himself at a dead-end or back where he started. The labyrinth toyed with his sanity, ensuring that every step he took was met with frustration and despair.

As Raymond traversed deeper into the heart of the labyrinth, he couldn't help but ponder the symbolism that surrounded him. The entangled trees and endless paths served as a reflection of his own tangled mind, its convoluted thoughts and fractured memories. Every twist and turn felt like a descent into the recesses of his consciousness, each step taking him further away from reality and deeper into his own delusions.

The forest came alive with haunting whispers that seemed to emanate from the very trees themselves. They echoed through Raymond's mind, their words teasing fragments of truth that danced just out of reach. He strained to make sense of them, desperate to unravel the enigma that had consumed him.

Raymond's journey through the labyrinth represented a battle against himself, a quest to navigate the maze of his own mind and confront the demons that haunted him. Each step brought him closer to the heart of his delusions, where the silver siren awaited, obscured by the fog of uncertainty and illusion.

As Raymond moved deeper into the labyrinth, time lost all meaning. The forest became an all-encompassing entity, its presence merging with his thoughts and fears. He pushed forward with a determination fueled by desperation, knowing that within the depths of this tangled maze lay answers that could either save him or unravel him completely.

With every footfall echoing in the silence that enveloped him, Raymond's resolve grew stronger. He would navigate this labyrinth, face the darkness within, and emerge on the other side. The journey was treacherous and uncertain, but he knew that only by delving into his own tangled psyche could he hope to find the truth and reclaim his sanity.

Raymond's breath quickened as something glimmered in the distance—a faint silver light that flickered amidst the shadows. With renewed vigor, he pushed through the underbrush, following the ethereal glow until he stood before a hidden clearing.

There, bathed in moonlight filtered through a canopy of leaves, stood the silver siren—her flowing gown shimmering in the darkness. Her features were obscured by a veil, leaving only her eyes visible—a piercing shade of silver that seemed to hold a multitude of secrets.

Raymond's heart pounded in his chest as he beheld the figure before him. In that moment, he knew that this encounter would be pivotal—an intersection between reality and delusion, truth and deception. He took a step forward, his voice trembling but filled with determination.

"Silver siren," Raymond called out, his words carrying a mixture of desperation and longing. "I've come to find the answers. Please, show me the way."

The silver siren's eyes bore into Raymond's, her gaze unfathomable and enigmatic. She reached out a slender hand, beckoning him closer. Despite the weight of uncertainty pressing upon him, Raymond moved towards her, drawn by an undeniable magnetic force.

As he stood face-to-face with the silver siren, their connection transcended words. In her gaze, Raymond saw flickers of recognition—perhaps a shared understanding of the pain and turmoil that had brought them together.

But as the forest whispered its secrets and shadows danced around them, Raymond couldn't shake the feeling that this encounter was merely one step on a treacherous path. The truth he sought might be closer than ever before, but it was clear that this dance with the silver siren would demand more than he could have ever anticipated.

With the silver siren at his side, Raymond braced himself for what lay ahead—the climax of his journey through madness and delusion—for in that tangled labyrinth, his fate and the fate of those he loved hung in precarious balance.

The truth awaited, hidden amidst the labyrinthine depths of Raymond's mind. And as he ventured further into the unknown, he remained determined to navigate its twists and turns, to confront his demons head-on, and to ultimately reclaim his shattered identity.

The forest was alive with an eerie stillness, the silence broken only by the sound of Raymond's rapid footsteps crunching on fallen leaves. Every breath felt heavy, as if the weight of his delusions bore down upon him. The dense foliage seemed to close in around him, obscuring his view and heightening his sense of unease.

Raymond's heart pounded in his chest as he stumbled through the maze-like undergrowth, searching for solace amidst the chaos within his mind. The forest whispered its secrets, haunting echoes that reverberated through his thoughts. Shadows danced along the forest floor, their ethereal movements mirroring the twisting labyrinth of his own delusions.

As he pressed deeper into the heart of the forest, Raymond's grip on reality grew increasingly tenuous. His mind spun with fragmented memories and twisted perceptions. He yearned for a glimpse of clarity, a respite from the torment that plagued him day and night.

Suddenly, a voice echoed through the trees, slicing through the oppressive silence. It was a whisper, barely audible but filled with an undeniable pull. Raymond followed the sound, his steps guided by an unseen force.

With each passing moment, the whispers grew louder, more distinct. They taunted him with cryptic messages and fragmented truths that danced just beyond his grasp. Raymond's pulse quickened as he drew closer to their source, anticipation mingling with apprehension.

And then, there she was—the silver siren emerged from the shadows, bathed in an ethereal glow that illuminated her graceful form. Her gown shimmered like moonlight on water, her eyes glinting with a mysterious intensity that held Raymond captive.

"Who are you?" he asked, his voice barely above a whisper. "What do you want from me?"

The silver siren smiled—her lips curling into a knowing grin. Her eyes bore into Raymond's soul, seeming to understand the depths of his despair. She reached out a hand, her touch as light as a whisper.

"I am the conduit between worlds," she whispered, her voice a melodic whisper that sent shivers down Raymond's spine. "I hold the truth you seek—the answers to unlock the prison within your mind."

Raymond's breath caught in his throat as hope flickered within him. Could this silver siren truly free him from the labyrinth of his own delusions? He had spent so long lost in the tangled web of his thoughts, desperate for redemption and release.

But doubt lingered at the edges of his mind, like tendrils of darkness threatening to consume him once more. Was the silver siren a harbinger of salvation or a temptress leading him further astray?

As he stood on the precipice between faith and skepticism, Raymond made a choice—a leap of faith. He took the silver siren's outstretched hand, intertwining their destinies.

Together, they ventured deeper into the forest—the whispers growing louder with each step. The path ahead remained uncertain, fraught with danger and uncertainty. But Raymond was no longer alone—guided by the enigmatic silver siren, he would face whatever lay ahead.

With each footfall echoing through the forest, Raymond's determination grew stronger. The silver siren's presence offered a glimmer of hope amidst the darkness of his mind. Together, they would navigate the twisted labyrinth and discover the truth that awaited—the key to unlocking Raymond's fragmented existence.

The forest around them seemed to pulse with energy, as if aware of their presence. Shadows danced and twisted, their movements mirroring the chaos within Raymond's mind. But now, armed with newfound purpose, he pressed forward, no longer afraid to confront his demons head-on.

As Raymond delved deeper into the heart of the forest, his journey mirrored the tumultuous battle raging within him. It was a battle for his sanity, a fight against the relentless grip of his own delusions. With every step, he grew closer to the truth—a truth that had the power to either set him free or consume him completely.

The whispers in the forest grew louder, their words intertwining with Raymond's thoughts. They beckoned him forward, urging him to embrace the unknown. And as the silver siren led the way, Raymond followed, ready to confront the darkness that awaited them both.

Raymond's breath quickened as something glimmered in the distance—a faint silver light that flickered amidst the shadows. With renewed vigor, he pushed through the underbrush, following the ethereal glow until he stood before a hidden clearing.

There, bathed in moonlight filtered through a canopy of leaves, stood the silver siren—her flowing gown shimmering in the darkness. Her features were obscured by a veil, leaving only her eyes visible—a piercing shade of silver that seemed to hold a multitude of secrets.

Raymond's heart pounded in his chest as he beheld the figure before him. In that moment, he knew that this encounter would be pivotal—an intersection between reality and delusion, truth and deception. He took a step forward, his voice trembling but filled with determination.

"Silver siren," Raymond called out, his words carrying a mixture of desperation and longing. "I've come to find the answers. Please, show me the way."

The silver siren's eyes bore into Raymond's, her gaze unfathomable and enigmatic. She reached out a slender hand, beckoning him closer. Despite the weight of uncertainty pressing upon him, Raymond moved towards her, drawn by an undeniable magnetic force.

As he stood face-to-face with the silver siren, their connection transcended words. In her gaze, Raymond saw flickers of recognition—perhaps a shared understanding of the pain and turmoil that had brought them together.

But as the forest whispered its secrets and shadows danced around them, Raymond couldn't shake the feeling that this encounter was merely one step on a treacherous path. The truth he sought might be closer than ever before, but it was clear that this dance with the silver siren would demand more than he could have ever anticipated.

With the silver siren at his side, Raymond braced himself for what lay ahead—the climax of his journey through madness and delusion—for in that tangled labyrinth, his fate and the fate of those he loved hung in precarious balance.

The truth awaited, hidden amidst the labyrinthine depths of Raymond's mind. And as he ventured further into the unknown, he remained determined to navigate its twists and turns, to confront his demons head-on, and to ultimately reclaim his shattered identity.

14

Entangled Deception

Shannon sat across from Blaise at a secluded location, their eyes filled with determination and a touch of apprehension. They had come together to share the information Shannon had obtained from the mysterious informant. The tension hung heavy in the air as they discussed their next moves, strategizing on how to protect themselves from the silver siren's web of deceit and manipulation.

The room they were in was dimly lit, casting long shadows that danced across the walls. It was a place where secrets were whispered and alliances forged in the darkness. Shannon glanced around, her gaze lingering on the hidden corners and concealed exits. She couldn't shake the feeling that they were being watched, that danger lurked just beyond their awareness.

"We have to be careful," Shannon said, her voice low yet steady. "The silver siren is more powerful than we anticipated. She has connections to influential individuals in the realm of psilocybin therapy."

Blaise nodded, his expression grave. "I've heard rumors about this network. They operate in the shadows, using their knowledge of hallucinogens to manipulate and control those who seek their assistance."

Shannon clenched her fist, frustration mingling with determination. "We can't let them continue exploiting vulnerable people for their own gain," she said. "We have to expose the truth and bring an end to their reign."

Silence settled between them as they contemplated the enormity of their task. The silver siren's web was intricate, stretching its tendrils far and wide. But Shannon refused to be intimidated.

"We need concrete evidence," Blaise finally broke the silence, his voice filled with resolve. "Something that will expose their crimes and ensure justice is served."

Shannon nodded in agreement. "I've been digging through old case files, trying to find a connection between the silver siren and those involved in psilocybin therapy," she said. "There has to be a way to unravel this web."

As they delved deeper into their discussion, Shannon and Blaise realized that their paths were intertwined, their fates inexorably linked. They were two souls bound by a common goal—to expose the silver siren's true identity and protect those who had fallen victim to her manipulation.

But even as they strategized, the weight of their task pressed upon them. The silver siren had proven herself to be cunning and elusive, always one step ahead. Shannon couldn't help but wonder if their efforts were in vain, if they were simply playing into the siren's hands.

"We can't let fear dictate our actions," Blaise said, his voice filled with conviction. "We have to stay one step ahead, anticipate her moves."

Shannon looked into his eyes, seeing a glimmer of hope amidst the uncertainty. They might be facing an adversary more powerful than they could have ever imagined, but they also possessed a determination that could not be extinguished.

"We'll navigate this treacherous game together," Shannon said, her voice steady with resolve. "As long as we trust each other and remain vigilant, we can unravel the silver siren's web."

Blaise reached across the table, placing his hand on top of Shannon's. Their connection felt electric—a symbol of solidarity in the face of darkness.

"We won't let her win," Blaise said, determination shining in his eyes. "We will find a way to protect those who have been ensnared by her illusions, no matter the cost."

As they sat in that dimly lit room, Shannon and Blaise knew that their fight had only just begun. The silver siren's web was vast and complex, but they refused to be entangled within it. With every moment that passed, their resolve grew stronger, forging a bond that would withstand any challenge.

Together, they would navigate the shadows, exposing the silver siren's true identity and bringing an end to her reign. The path ahead may be treacherous, but they were prepared to face whatever dangers awaited them—united in their pursuit of justice and truth.

Shannon felt a mix of excitement and trepidation as she stood outside the dimly lit café. The air was heavy with the scent of coffee and the low murmur of conversation. She took a deep breath, gathering her resolve before stepping inside.

As she entered the cozy establishment, Shannon's eyes scanned the room, searching for any signs of danger or surveillance. Satisfied that she had gone undetected, she made her way to a secluded booth in the corner. The candle on the table flickered, casting dancing shadows across her face.

Her heart raced with anticipation as she waited for her contact, the mysterious informant who claimed to hold vital information about the silver siren. Every creak of the chair and rustle of papers seemed to heighten the tension in the air.

And then, like a phantom emerging from the shadows, a figure approached her booth. Shannon's breath caught in her throat as their eyes met—a gaze filled with intensity and purpose. She recognized the wide-brimmed hat and scarf pulled up to their nose—the signature camouflage of her informant.

"Shannon Saunders?" the informant whispered, their voice barely audible over the ambient noise.

She nodded, her pulse quickening with a mixture of curiosity and caution. This was it—the moment she had been waiting for.

The informant slid into the seat opposite Shannon, their eyes never leaving hers. Their presence sent a shiver down her spine, a silent reminder of the dangers that lurked in their shared pursuit of the truth.

"I have information about the silver siren," the informant began, their voice dripping with secrets. "But before I tell you anything, you need to understand the danger you're putting yourself in."

Shannon leaned forward, her voice steady but tinged with urgency. "I'm aware of the risks," she replied. "But I need to know the truth."

The informant hesitated for a moment, their gaze searching Shannon's face as if weighing her commitment to the cause. Finally, they leaned back and began to speak, their words measured and filled with caution.

"The silver siren is more powerful than you can imagine," the informant whispered, their voice barely audible. "She has connections to influential individuals in the realm of psilocybin therapy—a web of manipulation and control that ensnares those who cross her path."

Shannon's eyes widened with realization. The pieces of the puzzle were finally coming together. Psilocybin therapy—the unique form of treatment involving hallucinogens—had always been at the heart of Raymond's disappearance and the silver siren's allure. But now she understood the depths of their connection, the danger that lay within the web of deception.

"We must tread carefully," the informant continued, their voice layered with caution. "The silver siren can blur the lines between reality and illusion. She will stop at nothing to protect her secrets."

Shannon nodded, her determination solidifying. She had always known that her pursuit of the truth would come with risks, but now she understood the full extent of the game she was playing. The stakes were higher than ever.

"What do you want in return for this information?" Shannon asked, her voice laced with resolve.

The informant smiled, a glint of mystery dancing in their eyes. "I'll tell you what you need to know," they said cryptically. "But first, you must promise to protect yourself and those close to you. This journey will be perilous, and you'll need all the allies you can find."

Shannon felt a surge of purpose welling within her. With this newfound ally by her side, she would navigate the treacherous path before her. The silver siren's web might be intricate, but she was determined to unravel its threads—one revelation at a time.

As they continued their conversation, Shannon and the informant delved deeper into the silver siren's origins and motivations. Each piece of information brought them closer to the truth, but also heightened their awareness of the danger that lay ahead.

Hours passed in a whirlwind of questions, revelations, and strategizing. The room seemed to hold its breath as they contemplated the magnitude of their task, their shared determination forging an unspoken bond between them.

"We can't let fear dictate our actions," Shannon said, her voice filled with conviction. "We have to stay one step ahead, anticipate the silver siren's moves."

The informant nodded, a flicker of hope in their eyes. "Together, we can expose her true identity and protect those who have fallen victim to her manipulations," they replied.

As Shannon looked into their eyes, she knew that this partnership would be pivotal—a beacon of light in the darkness that surrounded them. They might be facing an adversary more powerful than they could have ever imagined, but they possessed a determination that could not be extinguished.

"We won't let her win," Shannon vowed, her voice steady with resolve. "No matter the cost, we will bring an end to her reign."

With those words hanging in the air, Shannon and the informant left the café—two souls united in their pursuit of justice and truth. The path ahead was treacherous, but they were prepared to face whatever dangers awaited them. Together, they would navigate the shadows and unravel the silver siren's web—one revelation at a time.

15

Rescuing the Lost Soul

Shannon and Blaise found themselves standing outside the abandoned beach side estate, their breath visible in the cold night air. The moon cast an eerie glow over the dilapidated structure, its walls covered in ivy and worn by years of neglect. This was the lair of the silver siren—a place filled with danger and uncertainty.

They exchanged a determined glance, silently conveying their shared resolve. With night vision goggles securely in place, they approached the estate cautiously, their footsteps barely making a sound on the overgrown path.

As they reached the entrance, Shannon's heart pounded in her chest. She glanced at Blaise, witnessing a mix of excitement and apprehension mirrored in his eyes. They had strategized every move, studied blueprints, and memorized the layout of the lair. Now, it was time to put their plan into action.

Blaise knelt down in front of the locked door, his tools at the ready. Years of experience as a hacker had honed his skills, and he worked with precision to bypass the security system. Shannon kept watch, her senses heightened and alert for any sign of danger.

A soft click echoed through the night as Blaise successfully unlocked the door. They exchanged a knowing smile before stepping into the darkness beyond.

The air inside the lair carried a heavy, musty scent—a testament to its abandonment. Shadows danced on the walls, casting intricate patterns that seemed to flicker with a life of their own. Shannon's heartbeat quickened as she navigated through the dimly lit corridors, following Blaise's lead.

Suddenly, a startling clatter broke the silence—an unexpected trap sprung to deter intruders. Instinct kicked in as Shannon and Blaise leaped apart just in time, narrowly avoiding a hidden pitfall. Their hearts raced as they collectively sighed with relief, knowing that they had encountered only the first of many obstacles.

As they ventured deeper into the lair, the silver siren's tricks began to manifest. Illusions played with their minds, distorting their perceptions of reality. Walls seemed to close in and corridors twisted and turned, disorienting them at every corner.

But Shannon and Blaise refused to succumb to the siren's manipulations. They relied on their trust in one another, grounding themselves amidst the chaos. Each step brought them closer to their goal, their determination growing stronger with each passing challenge.

Finally, they reached the heart of the lair—a chamber cloaked in darkness and dripping with an eerie silence. The air buzzed with anticipation as they prepared for the ultimate confrontation. This was where Raymond was being held captive, where his rescue would solidify their victory over the silver siren.

Shannon and Blaise took a moment to steel themselves, drawing upon their inner strength and newfound understanding of one another. They knew that the battle ahead would be as much internal as it was external—a test of their resolve and resilience.

With one last glance, Shannon and Blaise braced themselves. They were ready to face the silver siren head-on, armed with the knowledge that they had come this far together. Their combined force would unleash a wave of light to counteract the darkness that had ensnared so many.

In that moment, as they stepped into the chamber, Shannon and Blaise embraced their destiny—defenders of truth, warriors against manipulation. And so, with unwavering conviction, they confronted the silver siren, ready to break free from her clutches once and for all.

The silver siren stood before them, her icy gaze fixed upon Shannon and Blaise. Her presence exuded power and control, but they refused to be swayed by her illusions. They knew that behind her facade of beauty lay a web of deceit that had ensnared countless souls.

Shannon's voice rang out, strong and resolute. "We've come to put an end to your reign of manipulation. Release Raymond now, or face the consequences!"

The silver siren's lips curled into a sinister smile. "You think you can defeat me? You're just pawns in my game, easily manipulated."

But Shannon and Blaise stood tall, locked in a united front. They had faced down their own fears and insecurities, finding strength in each other along the way.

Blaise spoke with conviction, his voice filled with determination. "We've seen through your illusions, and we won't be fooled anymore. Your web of lies ends here."

With each word, Shannon and Blaise took a step forward, closing in on the silver siren, their resolve unwavering. They could feel the power of their shared purpose coursing through their veins, pushing them forward despite the fear that threatened to hold them back.

The air crackled with electricity as the standoff continued. The silver siren attempted to destabilize them, using her powers of manipulation to shatter their confidence. But Shannon and Blaise held strong, refusing to let doubt cloud their minds.

In a moment of clarity, Shannon saw through the silver siren's façade—a wounded soul who had succumbed to her own desire for power. With empathy in her voice, she spoke directly to the silver siren.

"We know the pain that drives you," Shannon said. "But we also know that there is another way. Release Raymond from your grasp, and we will help you find the healing you need."

For a fleeting moment, doubt flickered in the silver siren's eyes—a glimmer of vulnerability hidden beneath her icy exterior. But then, her features hardened once more, and she unleashed a wave of power that sent Shannon and Blaise reeling.

As they struggled to regain their footing, Shannon and Blaise locked eyes. Their connection sparked with determination, a silent message passing between them—a reminder of their shared purpose and the strength they had found in each other.

Together, they channeled their own inner power, refusing to be overwhelmed by the silver siren's influence. With newfound resolve, Shannon and Blaise fought back, their combined force radiating through the chamber.

The confrontation reached its climax as the silver siren's power faltered under the weight of Shannon and Blaise's determination. With one final push, they shattered her illusions, revealing the truth hidden beneath her manipulative facade.

As the silver siren crumbled before them, releasing Raymond from her grasp, Shannon and Blaise felt a wave of relief wash over them. They had succeeded in their mission—to free Raymond from the clutches of darkness and to break the surface of deception that had ensnared so many.

In the aftermath of their victory, Shannon helped Raymond to his feet, embracing him with tears in her eyes. Blaise stood by their side, a silent witness to the power of friendship and the strength that came from facing their fears head-on.

Together, they emerged from the lair of the silver siren, bathed in the light of a new beginning. The journey had been perilous, but it had also forged an unbreakable bond between Shannon, Blaise, and Raymond—one that would carry them forward as they unraveled the silver siren's secrets and began the process of healing and self-discovery.

The path ahead remained uncertain, filled with challenges yet to come. But as Shannon looked at her companions, she knew that they were no longer alone in their quest. Together, they would navigate the treacherous waters that lay ahead, ready to face whatever obstacles came their way.

16

Unmasking the Hidden Scheme: Shannon Exposes a Far-reaching Conspiracy in Psilocybin Therapy

Shannon and Blaise sat hunched over their laptops in a dimly lit room, their eyes fixed on the encrypted messages Raymond had left behind. The air was thick with anticipation as they meticulously deciphered each symbol and code, their minds racing to unveil the hidden connection between the tech tycoon and psilocybin therapy.

As Shannon's fingers flew across the keyboard, Blaise leaned in closer, his breath quickening with every revelation. He marveled at Shannon's tenacity and determination, her unwavering focus evident in every keystroke.

Hours turned into days as they delved deeper into the codes, unraveling the hidden meaning behind each message. The room around them faded away, replaced by a singular purpose—to expose the truth. With each decrypted message, they unearthed fragments of a larger puzzle—a web of manipulation and exploitation that stretched far beyond their initial suspicions.

Finally, Shannon sat back, her eyes gleaming with a mix of excitement and trepidation. "I think I've cracked it," she said, her voice laden with anticipation.

Blaise leaned closer, his heart racing. "What does it say?"

Shannon took a deep breath before speaking. "These messages reveal a secret alliance between the tech tycoon and powerful individuals in the realm of psilocybin therapy. It seems they have been using this unique form of therapy as a means to manipulate vulnerable individuals and control their perceptions."

Blaise's eyes widened in disbelief. "So, the tech tycoon isn't just involved in exploiting people through his tech empire—he's also using these healing practices for his own gain?"

Shannon nodded solemnly. "It seems that way. This goes beyond Raymond's disappearance; we've stumbled upon a conspiracy that extends its tendrils into the realm of power and influence."

The weight of their findings settled heavily on their shoulders, but neither Shannon nor Blaise wavered in their resolve. The truth needed to be unveiled, regardless of the personal risks they were taking.

As days turned into weeks, Shannon and Blaise delved deeper into the heart of the conspiracy. They pored over documents, interviewed experts in the field, and sought out testimonies from those who had fallen victim to the tech tycoon's manipulations. With each new piece of evidence, their conviction grew stronger, fueling their determination to expose the truth.

Finally, Shannon paused, her eyes fixed on a particularly damning email chain. Her breath caught in her throat as she read through the messages—a disturbing web of connections between the tech tycoon and other influential figures in the industry.

"We can't let this go unnoticed," Shannon said firmly, her voice laced with determination. "We have a moral obligation to bring justice to those affected by these unethical practices."

Blaise's gaze never wavered from Shannon's face as he nodded in agreement. "We've come too far to turn back now. We hold the power to dismantle this network of corruption."

With renewed purpose, Shannon and Blaise continued their investigation, knowing that their actions could bring about profound change. They knew there would be risks along the way—dangers lurking in the shadows—but they refused to let fear dictate their actions.

Together, they prepared to confront the silver siren—the enigmatic figure at the center of the conspiracy. Their hearts pounded with adrenaline as they braced themselves for what lay ahead. This was no longer just about Raymond; it was about justice for all those impacted by this insidious web of manipulation. And together, they would fight for that justice, unveiling the truth and breaking free from the clutches of darkness that had ensnared so many innocent lives.

17

The Unmasking: Shannon exposes the dark truth behind the Psilocybin therapy program.

Shannon's heart pounded in her chest as she stood face-to-face with the tech tycoon, her palms slick with nervous sweat. The room fell into an expectant silence, all eyes trained on the confrontation taking place before them. Shannon took a deep breath, steeling herself for the battle that lay ahead.

"I have evidence," Shannon stated, her voice filled with conviction and determination. "Evidence that implicates you in the exploitation of vulnerable individuals through unauthorized psilocybin therapy practices."

The tech tycoon's gaze flickered with a mix of defiance and uncertainty. His carefully constructed mask of power began to crack under the weight of Shannon's allegations. He attempted to regain his composure, but his voice trembled slightly as he spoke.

"These are baseless accusations," he spat, attempting to dismiss Shannon's claims. "I assure you, my practices are within the boundaries of ethical and legal guidelines."

Shannon held her ground, unflinching in the face of his denial. With a calm resolve, she presented the recorded conversations she had meticulously gathered—proof of his direct involvement in manipulating vulnerable individuals for personal gain.

Gasps rippled through the crowd as they absorbed the damning evidence. The room was charged with tension as attendees grappled with the truth they had just witnessed. The tech tycoon's once-confident façade faltered, leaving him exposed and vulnerable.

"I trusted you," Shannon continued, her voice tinged with anger and sadness. "But trust has its limits when it comes at the expense of innocent lives."

As Shannon spoke, tears welled in her eyes, reflecting the pain and betrayal she felt on behalf of every person who had fallen victim to the tech tycoon's unethical practices. The weight of their stories hung heavily in the air—a reminder of the immense power held by those in positions of influence.

The tech tycoon surveyed the sea of faces before him, realizing that his empire was on the brink of collapse. The room murmured with whispered conversations, attendees reevaluating their own beliefs and experiences. Questions swirled through their minds as they contemplated the broader implications of unchecked innovation.

In this moment, Shannon's words resonated with the crowd. She had given voice to their concerns and ignited a spark of collective action. The power dynamics were shifting, and the attendees began to question not only the tech tycoon's actions but also the system that allowed such exploitation to thrive.

With a determined expression, Shannon addressed the conference attendees, raising her voice above the hum of conversation. "We must demand accountability from those in power," she implored. "Only through transparency and ethical practices can we ensure the well-being of vulnerable individuals seeking healing."

The crowd erupted into applause, a chorus of support for Shannon's call to action. Even amidst the chaos and uncertainty, hope glimmered in their eyes—the hope that change was possible, that justice could be served.

As security guards approached to escort the tech tycoon out of the venue, the conference-goers' demands for justice grew louder. The tide had shifted, and the previously untouchable figure now faced the consequences of his actions.

Shannon stood tall, a beacon of resilience and strength amidst the tumultuous sea of voices. She knew that her work had only just begun—that there were more battles to fight and more stories to uncover. But in this moment, she allowed herself a flicker of satisfaction, knowing that she had exposed the truth and set in motion a wave of change that would resonate far beyond this conference.

She turned to face Blaise, who stood beside her throughout the confrontation, his expression a mix of pride and admiration. Their shared journey had led them to this pivotal moment—a moment when they realized the power they held to challenge corruption and fight for justice.

As they stepped out of the conference hall, the weight of their actions settled upon their shoulders. They knew that the road ahead would be filled with challenges and risks, but they were prepared to face whatever obstacles came their way.

This was just the beginning—a catalyst for change that would ripple through the industry and impact the lives of those who had been manipulated and exploited. With renewed determination, Shannon and Blaise vowed to continue their fight, shedding light on other instances of exploitation within the industry and bringing justice to those affected.

As they walked away from the conference venue, a sense of purpose and hope filled their hearts. They may have confronted one tech tycoon, but their battle against corruption had only just begun. And together, they would be a force to be reckoned with—a beacon of truth in a world that desperately needed it.

18

Bound by the Journey

Shannon and Blaise found themselves sitting on a secluded bench overlooking the ocean, the sound of crashing waves providing a soothing backdrop to their conversation. The salty breeze carried a sense of peace and tranquility as they took in the breathtaking view before them.

As they sat side by side, their fingers intertwined, Shannon turned to Blaise with a gentle smile. "I never thought I would find solace and healing in nature like this," she whispered, her voice filled with gratitude. "But being here with you, it feels like all the weight has been lifted off my shoulders."

Blaise squeezed Shannon's hand, his gaze fixed on the horizon. "Nature has a way of grounding us," he replied softly. "It reminds us of our place in the world and helps us find clarity amidst the chaos. I'm glad we could share this moment together."

In the serene silence that followed, Shannon closed her eyes and let the sun's warmth wash over her. She felt a renewed sense of hope and purpose blossoming within her, nourished by the beauty that surrounded them. Thoughts of their journey flashed through her mind—every sleepless night, every breakthrough, every moment of doubt overcome.

"You know," Shannon began, her voice barely above a whisper, "when we first started this investigation, I was driven by anger and a thirst for justice. But along the way, something shifted within me. I realized that compassion and empathy were just as important in the pursuit of truth."

Blaise nodded, his eyes reflecting understanding. "I've seen that transformation in you," he said gently. "You've shown me the power of vulnerability and how it can create profound connections with others. Your dedication to seeking justice is fueled by an unwavering belief in the value of every individual's story."

A soft smile tugged at the corners of Shannon's lips as she looked at Blaise. "And what about you?" she asked, her voice filled with genuine curiosity. "What have you learned about yourself through this journey?"

Blaise's gaze turned inward for a moment before he turned to Shannon, his eyes sparkling with newfound introspection. "I've realized that it's okay to need stability in my life," he confessed, his voice tinged with vulnerability. "For so long, I've been running away from commitments and seeking adventure in every corner of the world. But being with you, I've found a sense of grounding—a place where I can be myself without fear."

Shannon's heart swelled with affection as she listened to Blaise's words. In his vulnerability, she saw strength and growth—a testament to their shared journey of healing and self-discovery.

As they sat there, enveloped by the beauty of nature, their connection deepened. They had become each other's pillars of support, their shared experiences forging an unbreakable bond. The weight of their pasts no longer burdened them; instead, it lifted them higher, propelling them towards the future they both yearned for.

With each passing moment, Shannon and Blaise's souls danced in harmony with the rhythm of the waves. This moment was a celebration of their resilience and courage—two individuals who had braved the darkest corners of their own hearts and emerged stronger and more compassionate.

Their time on the bench stretched into infinity, a pause in the grand symphony of life. And as they held each other's hands and gazed out into the vast expanse of the ocean, they knew that they were exactly where they were meant to be—side by side, writing their own story of healing and love against the backdrop of an ever-changing world.

In that moment, Shannon felt a profound sense of gratitude for everything they had endured—the challenges, the pain, and even the moments of doubt. It had all led them here, to this moment of healing and connection.

As the sun began its descent, casting a warm golden glow over the ocean, Shannon leaned her head against Blaise's shoulder. They watched as the sky transformed into hues of orange and pink, their silhouettes merging against the vibrant backdrop.

In the peaceful tranquility of that moment, they embraced the present and looked forward to the future, confident that whatever challenges lay ahead, they would face them together. Love and resilience filled their hearts, guiding them towards an uncertain but hopeful tomorrow.

Their journey was far from over, but with each other by their side, Shannon and Blaise knew they had the strength and determination to navigate whatever came their way. And as they sat there, entwined in each other's arms, the world seemed more beautiful, more vibrant than ever before.

In this quiet embrace, they found solace and hope—a respite from the chaos of their past and a promise of a brighter future. And as they watched the sun dip below the horizon, leaving behind a trail of shimmering light on the water, Shannon whispered words filled with love and gratitude.

"Thank you," she said softly, her voice both a promise and a declaration. "Thank you for helping me find healing amidst the storms. Together, we can face anything."

Blaise pressed a gentle kiss to Shannon's temple, his touch a testament to their shared journey. "Together," he echoed, his voice filled with unwavering certainty. "Always."

And so, as the colors of the setting sun painted the sky with their brilliance, Shannon and Blaise embraced their future—one filled with love, healing, and endless possibilities.

19

Healing the Shadows

Shannon and Blaise found themselves sitting in the waiting room of Dr. Elizabeth Sullivan, a renowned therapist specializing in trauma and healing., the anticipation hanging heavy in the air. With each breath they took, they felt a mixture of nerves and excitement coursing through their veins. This session marked a pivotal moment in Raymond's healing journey—a chance for him to face his past traumas head-on and find redemption.

Dr. Elizabeth Sullivan, a compassionate and experienced therapist, welcomed Shannon, Blaise, and Raymond with a warm smile. Her presence radiated a sense of reassurance amidst the uncertainty of what lay ahead.

"Raymond," Dr. Sullivan began gently, her voice laced with empathy. "Today, we're going to delve deep into your past traumas. It won't be easy, but it's a crucial step towards finding healing and reclaiming your sense of self."

Raymond nodded, his eyes filled with a mix of determination

and trepidation. He knew that this session would challenge him to confront painful memories he had long buried. But with Shannon and Blaise by his side, he felt a glimmer of hope—a belief that he no longer had to face this darkness alone.

Dr. Sullivan guided Raymond through a series of exercises designed to unlock the depths of his suppressed memories. She encouraged him to close his eyes and focus on his breath, grounding himself in the present moment.

As Raymond delved into his memories, emotions washed over him like crashing waves against a shore. Tears streamed down his face as he vividly recounted moments of neglect and abuse that had haunted him for years. Shannon reached out and gently squeezed his hand, offering unwavering support in this vulnerable moment.

With Dr. Sullivan's guidance, Raymond began to navigate the intricate webs of trauma woven into his psyche. Each memory unearthed another piece of the puzzle—a painful mosaic of betrayal and loss.

Throughout the session, Shannon listened intently, her heart breaking for the pain Raymond had endured. She marveled at his courage and resilience, admiring his ability to face his past head-on. In those moments, she saw the true depth of Raymond's strength—a testament to the power of human resilience in the face of adversity.

Dr. Sullivan provided guidance and reassurance, reminding Raymond that healing was within reach—that he had the power to shape his own narrative and find a path towards self-compassion. She emphasized the importance of patience and self-care throughout this arduous process.

As the session drew to a close, Raymond opened his eyes, finding solace in the supportive gazes of Shannon and Blaise. They had witnessed his vulnerability, his rawest self laid bare, and yet they remained by his side—proof that he was not alone in this journey.

"Thank you," Raymond whispered, his voice filled with gratitude and a renewed sense of hope. "Thank you for guiding me through this darkness and helping me find my way towards light."

Shannon smiled warmly, her eyes shining with pride. "You're stronger than you realize," she said softly. "Together, we'll continue to navigate this path of healing—supporting each other every step of the way."

Blaise wrapped an arm around Raymond's shoulder, offering silent encouragement. "You've shown incredible resilience," he said sincerely. "Remember that your past doesn't define you. It's what you do with your present that matters most."

Raymond nodded, a newfound determination etched onto his features. With this session behind him, he knew that he had taken a significant step towards closure and redemption. The road ahead may be challenging, but he was no longer weighed down by the chains of his past.

As they left Dr. Sullivan's office, Shannon, Blaise, and Raymond walked hand in hand—united in their shared commitment to healing and growth. The sun shone brightly overhead, casting warm rays of hope on their path.

In this moment, they understood that closure and redemption were not far-fetched ideals—they were tangible realities waiting to be claimed. And together, they were brave enough to face the shadows of the past, knowing that in doing so, they would unlock a brighter and more fulfilling future.

20

A Ripple of Hope

Shannon stood on the Malibu coastline, her gaze fixed on the horizon as the sun began to rise. The sky was painted in hues of pink and orange, casting a warm glow over the crashing waves. In this fleeting moment of tranquility, she couldn't help but reflect on the profound journey she had embarked upon—a journey that had led her to uncover Raymond's hidden past and confront the demons that haunted him.

As the sun continued its ascent, Shannon took a deep breath, allowing the salty ocean breeze to cleanse her spirit. The weight of everything she had experienced throughout this investigation hung heavy in the air, but so did a sense of possibility and renewal. She had witnessed firsthand the transformative power of empathy and understanding—how it could heal deep-seated wounds and ignite positive change.

Her fiery red hair shimmered in the golden morning light, giving her an ethereal glow as she contemplated the path ahead. Shannon recognized the growth and transformation she herself had undergone during this tumultuous journey. No longer just an overreaching television reporter hungry for sensational stories, she had evolved into a compassionate seeker of truth—a woman unafraid to confront darkness and uncover hidden stories.

With each new dawn, Shannon's conviction grew stronger. She vowed to carry on Raymond's legacy, using her words to expose hidden truths, empower others, and advocate for justice. She understood the immense power storytelling held—a tool that could bridge gaps, cultivate empathy, and ignite conversations that would bring about meaningful change.

The rising sun cast a warm glow over Shannon's features as she continued to contemplate her future journalistic endeavors. She knew that Raymond's disappearance was just the beginning—a catalyst for greater understanding and healing. Armed with the knowledge she had gained and the connections she had forged, she was determined to continue shining a light on injustices, no matter how daunting the path ahead might be.

In this moment of stillness and introspection, Shannon couldn't help but feel an overwhelming sense of gratitude. She was grateful for the opportunity to have played a role in Raymond's healing journey, grateful for the support and love that had sustained her throughout this investigation, and grateful for the unwavering resilience of the human spirit.

As the waves crashed against the shore, Shannon found solace in their rhythm. Each wave symbolized closure and redemption—tangible realities waiting to be claimed. She knew the road ahead would be filled with challenges, but she also knew she was not alone. The vast expanse of the ocean echoed her determination, reminding her that every step forward mattered.

With a renewed sense of purpose, Shannon turned away from the shoreline, ready to embrace what lay beyond the waves. The sky beckoned her forward, casting its warm glow of possibility upon her path. And as she took her first steps, she carried with her the strength and determination to make a difference—one story at a time.

About the Author

T. S. Dunne was born in Florida in 1974, into a loving family, and was raised with one older sister. In 1992, T. S. moved to the Northeast to attend college. In 1994, T.S. lived in the United Kingdom and enrolled at Balliol College in Oxford. Later in the year, T. S. met his father, and the two traveled the southern half of Ireland together. T. S. resided in Galway and took boat trips out to explore the Aran Islands, where he would hike to the chair of one of his favorite writers, John Millington Synge, on Inishmaan, to pray.

Back in America, T. S. graduated from college and continue to write poetry and cinematic fiction while residing in the Greenwich Village neighborhood of New York City, West Hollywood, California, and Key West, Florida. In 2010, he married his bride on the beach. T. S. and his wife welcomed their first child, a son, in 2012. In 2014, T. S. welcomed the birth of his new daughter. Also in 2014, T. S. was invited to Bosnia and Herzegovina to present on a special assignment. T. S. took residence in Paris in 2017, writing from the Saint Michel neighborhood, witnessing the beauty of the Notre Dame Cathedral, only months before the destructive inferno. Today, T. S. lives and writes throughout

Florida.

Also by T.S. Dunne

The Storm Within

2022 International #1 Best Seller in the following Amazon categories: Spiritual Healing, Men's Christian Living, Catholism Self Help, Christian Leadership, Christian Counseling, Christian Stewardship Christian Faith & Faith and Spirituality.

Silver Siren: A California Mystery

In the heart of Los Angeles, a young woman named Jacki gets caught up in a world of bank robberies and big waves. As she navigates the dangerous underbelly of the city, she must confront her own past and discover her true identity. Accompanied by the , this thrilling California story takes readers on a journey filled with love, deception, and redemption. With themes of trauma, identity, and personal growth, readers will be captivated by this gripping tale that keeps them hooked until the very end.

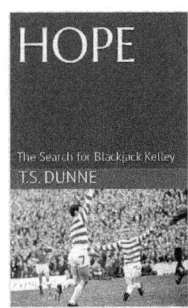

Hope: The Search for Blackjack Kelley

"The Legend of Blackjack Kelley" is a gripping tale that takes readers on a captivating journey through family secrets, redemption, and the search for identity. Emmet Kelley embarks on a mission to uncover the truth about his late father, a legendary figure in Irish football and a member of the Irish Republican Army. Set against the contrasting backdrops of Florida's sunny beaches and Ireland's rugged hills, this story weaves together elements of sports, historical events, and forbidden love. As Emmet delves deeper into his father's past, he discovers a complex web of intrigue and danger that leads to an unexpected and emotional reunion. With its rich exploration of Irish culture and history, this book offers readers a compelling and inspiring narrative that leaves them filled with hope and satisfaction.

In the Shadow of the Troubles: One Family's Struggle with the Past.

In the late 1970s, former Irish footballer "BlackJack" Kelly became entangled in the IRA, setting off a chain of tragic events that continue to haunt his family. Decades later, his son Emmet, unaware of his true heritage, travels from America to Ireland to meet his long-lost father. Set against a backdrop of political turmoil and family secrets, this gripping saga delves into the personal toll of violence and the enduring power of family ties. With its profound exploration of identity and the consequences of choices, this emotionally charged tale will leave readers captivated until the very end.